E-Z DICKENS SUPERHERO BOOK TWO:

THE THREE

Cathy McGough

Stratford Living Publishing

Contents

Dedication

For Tanja

EPILOGUE

AFTER A FEW BUSY days, E-Z finally got a good night's sleep. He dreamed about playing baseball and the next day Arden and PJ came by to take him to a game. "I'm not into playing today, but I'll come along for morale," he said.

"Sure thing," his friends replied.

Once they got E-Z onto the field, they insisted he play. They needed him to catch, and he agreed. When it came his first time to be at bat, He wanted to hit for himself. He grabbed his favourite bat and wheeled himself up to the plate. The first pitch was high, and he missed it. His pitching zone was really condensed since he was sitting down.

"Strike one," the umpire called out.

E-Z wheeled himself away from the plate. He took a couple more practice swings, then went back again. The next pitch he connected with it, and it fouled out.

"Strike two," the umpire called.

"No batter, no batter," the guys in the field chattered.

The pitcher threw a curve ball and E-Z leaned into the pitch and connected. It flew, out of the field. Over the fence. Out of the park.

"Take the bases," the umpire said. "You deserve it kid."

E-Z wheeled himself around the bases, holding back his chair from taking flight. When his chair connected with home plate, his teammates gathered around him cheering. He enjoyed it while it lasted.

Until he landed back inside the metal container again – only this time he was rolled up in a ball – and he was chair-less. Like a newborn babe, he breathed deeply as it was the only thing he could do. Wait. Babies could turn themselves over. All he had to do was concentrate, focus.

Yes, he did it. Only problem was, he wasn't any better off. He was still rolled up, in darkness. Confined in a space without light or opportunity to move hardly at all. In fact, the shape of the metal container was different this time. It was slenderer at the one end, shaped like a bullet.

Knowing this didn't help as his claustrophobia and anxiety kicked into high gear. He wondered how long he could keep breathing in this confined space. Not long. He'd run out of air in no time, and he'd die. He inhaled deeply, trying to keep the anxiety level down.

One thing was certain, there was no way Eriel could fit in this thing with him. Unless he blew the walls wide open – which might not be such a bad idea.

E-Z knocked on the walls and the ceiling. He yelled. Screamed. He remembered his phone. Could he reach it? It wasn't there. He'd put it into the sports bag to follow the no phones allowed on the field rule.

Outside of the container, there were troubling sounds. Scratching. Rats? No, not rats. He could deal with many things, but not rats. "Let's me out!" he screamed.

An engine started up. An older vehicle, like a truck. The floor beneath him began to shake and rattle as the bullet rolled forward and bounced around.

Outside the container was bouncing off the walls. Inside, he was in such a confined space there wasn't much movement. That was one advantage for being trapped in a bullet.

The vehicle hit something, and E-Z's head connected with the top of the thing. He cried out, but the sound died away. The metal container moved again, sideways. It hit something, then returned to its original position. His shoulder ached from the impact.

E-Z wondered if this was an Eriel task but decided it couldn't be. He began to conclude that he had been kidnapped and was being held captive. But why now?

"Hey!" he shouted as the metal object rolled about and landed on the flat bottom – where his bottom was. Now the weight was dispersed more evenly. He was comfortable. Or as comfortable as he could be under the circumstances. So, he remained very still until the vehicle came to a full stop and he went over end on end.

He took a deep breath, quieted himself, and said the words aloud,

"Roch-Ah-Or, A, Ra-Du, EE, El."

As he waited, he asked, "Where are you, Eriel?

Roch-Ah-Or, A, Ra-Du, EE, El?"

"You summoned me?" Eriel said. His voice was crisp and clear, but he was not visible.

"Yes, Eriel, I think I've been kidnapped. I'm in a container. Can you help me?"

"I know where you are always," Eriel said. "The question you should be asking is WILL I help you."

"I didn't know you had me under surveillance 24-7!" E-Z exclaimed, growing angrier as every moment passed. He took a few deep breaths and calmed himself down. He needed Eriel's help, and the archangel wasn't going to make it easy for him. "I can't see the driver of this thing and I can't extend my wings. And where is my chair? I'm running out of air in here. If you want me to finish those trials for you, then you better get me out of here and quickly."

"First you insult me, by questioning whether I am angel or not, then you beg me to help you. Humans are very fickle creatures indeed."

"I know. I'm sorry. Please help me."

"Have you considered," Eriel suggested. "That this IS a trial? Something which you must overcome yourself?"

"Are you telling me, this is definitely a trial?"

"I'm not saying it is. And I'm not saying it isn't," Eriel said with a snicker.

E-Z was fuming. He so missed Hadz and Reiki.

"So sad you still think about those two idiots. Now E-Z, if it were a trial, then how would you get yourself out of it?"

"First of all, they came through for me when you nearly killed the earth. Secondly, it cannot be a trial because there is no one for me to help."

Eriel laughed. "You consider yourself to be no one?" Eriel paused. "Today you are saving yourself and only yourself. Use the tools at your disposal." He hesitated then laughed again. "Think outside of the metal container." He laughter was so loud inside the metal bullet that it hurt E-Z's ears. He covered them. Then he heard Eriel no more.

E-Z closed his eyes and concentrated. He decided to ball up his fists and try to push the walls apart. No matter how hard he tried they would not budge. Plan B was to summon his chair which he did. He imagined it wasn't far away. Was it hovering above, waiting for E-Z to call it forth? He was concentrating so hard on calling his chair, that he didn't realize someone was walking outside. Footsteps on the pavement. One man, boots pounding. The man was making his way around the vehicle, to the back. A key went in. The door rolled up.

"He's been rolling around in here," the man said.

A laugh. Not Eriel's laugh. Another man's laugh.

Then a scream.

Then more screams.

Then running. Running away.

More screams.

Then movement. The container moving. Being lifted into his wheelchair.

Then going upwards, higher, and higher. Away to safety.

"Thank you," E-Z said to his chair. "Now take me home to Uncle Sam."

E-Z knew Uncle Sam would be able to get him out of the container. He'd need a giant can opener, but if there was one to be had, Uncle Sam would find it.

His wheelchair though sped off in the opposite direction.

CHAPTER ONE

F AR, FAR AWAY FROM where E-Z Dickens lived, a little girl danced. Her ballet lessons were in a small studio in the central business district of The Netherlands.

She was a pretty child, with golden hair, and a line of freckles stretching across her nose and cheeks. Her most memorable features were her hazel green eyes. The colour was the exact same as her Grandmama's. Her dream was to one day be The Netherlands' most famous ballet dancer

Her pink tutu was made from tulle. It was a net-like, light weight fabric used by designers for professional dancers. Her tutu had been designed and sewn for her by her nanny. The costume - a work of art in itself - so much so that every child in the class wanted one.

Hannah, Lia's Nanny received many requests from other parents to make their daughters the same tutu. She firmly told the children, their parents, teachers, and many others, that she didn't have time to take on the extra work. Although she could have used the money.

Everything Hannah did, she did because she loved her ward, Lia. Lia, who she called her kleintje which translated means little one.

With the balletles (translated: ballet class) nearly over, Lia packed her shoes away. She rubbed her sore feet.

All balletdansers (translated: ballet dancers) – even seven-year-olds like Lia needed to train for a minimum of twenty hours per week.

This added work, on top of a full school curriculum required dedication and commitment. Any children who could keep up, were promptly shown the door. No matter how much money their parents offered to pay to keep them in the program.

Lia hoped to one day meet her idol Igone de Jongh the most famous Netherland's ballet dancer of all time. Since her idol retired, Lia watched her performances on television.

Hannah looked after Lia on weekdays. Lia's mother Samantha travelled for business during the week.

Outside the dance studio, Hannah and Lia got into the Volkswagen Golf. They'd soon be home.

"Do you have any homework?" Hannah asked.

Lia nodded.

"Goed," translated as good. "Go and get started when I prepare dinner," Hannah said.

"Oke," translated as okay, Lia replied.

Lia at once went to her room where she hung up her ballet outfit, then got down to work at her desk.

At school they were learning about the legend of the The Witch Tree. Their task was to draw the tree and create something magical about it. She intended to draw an outline with chalk. Then use pipe cleaners for the roots and glitter on the leaves for the magical element.

Although she had a natural talent for art, she did not enjoy creating it. Her preference was for dance. She did not complain or dismiss tasks she didn't particularly like. It wasn't in her nature to be disobedient or disruptive.

Although Lia lived in Zumbert, Netherlands, she attended an international school. Her English was excellent. Zumbert itself was renown the world over as the birthplace of Vincent Van Gogh. Lia knew all about Van Gogh since she and he had the same blood running through their veins.

After completing her homework, she opened her computer. She on and played a game. Reaching the next level would only take a few moments. Hannah would soon be calling her down for avondeten (dinner.)

No one need ever know, a tiny voice in the back of her mind said. Lia listened to the voice, but to make sure no one did find out, she closed her bedroom door.

As her fingers clicked across the keyboard the lightbulb above her desk went out with a pop. She closed the laptop and opened her door again. She looked down the hall to where the spare halogen lightbulbs were. Nanny kept a supply in the linen cupboard at the top of the stairs. All Lia needed to do was zip out, fetch one, come back and change the lightbulb herself. Then she'd have more time to play her game.

Back in her room, she assessed the situation. She had to stand on her desk chair – which was on casters. She'd push it up firmly against the bed, to secure it. Yes, that would work.

The chair secured under the light fixture she climbed up onto it. Holding the new lightbulb under her chin she unscrewed the old one. The burned-out lightbulb she tossed onto the bed. Taking the other lightbulb from under her chin, she screwed it in.

CRACK!

The new lightbulb exploded.

Shards of glass, mostly minute in size sprayed out from it. Into the little girl's face and eyes.

Lia did not scream straightaway, for a blue light filled the room causing time to stand still. The light surrounded her as it moved up level with her face.

SWISH!

A tiny angelic creature appeared who examined the little girl's eyes. Then deciding they were damaged beyond repair she whispered, "Will you be, one of the three?"

"Ja," translated as yes, Lia said. as time stopped.

The angel, whose name was Haniel arrived. She sang a soothing lullaby to Lia, while she removed the glass.

In English, the song lyrics were:

"A sorrowful sad little girl sat down

Upon the riverbank.

The girl was weeping out of grief

Because both her parents were dead."

In Dutch, the song lyrics were:

"Asn d'oever van de snelle vliet

Eeen treurig meisje zat.

Het meisje huilde van verdriet

Omdat zij geen ouders meer had."

Fortunately, little Lia was sleeping so could not be frightened by the words of the lullaby.

When Haniel finished dealing with the worst part of Lia's wounds, she put her hands on her hips and stopped singing. Task nearly complete, all she had to do now was to lay the foundations for her protégé's new eyes.

Lia's two little hands were rolled up in balls. Tight little fists. Haniel allowed her wings to gently caress the closed fingers, coaxing them open.

When Lia's palms were open, the angel Haniel, using her index finger, outlined the shape of an eye on both palms. On the fingers, she drew one single line on each, leading from the palm up to the end of the finger. Her task completed, the angel Haniel, gently kissed Lia on the forehead, then with a

SWISH!

as she disappeared.

Time restarted and our brave little Lia still did not scream. Shock does that to your body as a defense mechanism and by stopping time, the pain also halted. When Lia finally screamed, she couldn't stop. Not when the ambulance arrived. Or when she was lifted out on a stretcher into the vehicle with siren joining in her chorus of screams. Or when she was pushed on a gurney into the hospital. Not when they shone a big light into her face, which she could feel but not see.

She did stop screaming when they sedated her. Then they used the latest technology to remove the remaining glass. However, every piece of glass had already been removed. The surgeons went ahead and bandaged her eyes then took her to her room to recover.

After the operation, Lia's mother Samantha arrived. She'd caught a red eye flight from London. She met the surgeon while her daughter slept on.

"I'm sorry, but she'll never see again," he said.

Lia's mother thrust her fist into her mouth fighting back the urge to wail.

The doctor said, "She can learn braille, and attend a school for the visually impaired. She's at an excellent age for learning and she'll soak up knowledge. In no time at all signing will be second nature for her."

"But my daughter wants to be a ballet dancer. Have you ever seen or heard of a blind professional dancer?"

"Alicia Alonso was partially blind. She didn't let it hold her back."

Lia's mother patted her sleeping daughter's hand. "Thank you, I'll find out details about her on the internet. Seven is far too young to be forced to give up on a dream."

"I agree. Now you get some rest too. Lia should be waking up soon and she'll need you to be strong for her. For when you tell her. If you'd like me to be here, too, let me know."

"Thank you, Doctor, I'll try to manage it myself first."

As the door closed, Lia's mother touched the marks on her daughter's face. The impressions left looked like angry raindrops. Then she looked at Lia's sleeping nanny Hannah. As she passed by her to get some water, she accidentally on purpose kicked her left shoe to wake her up. "Outside!" she said, as Hannah yawned.

Now in the hallway, Lia's mother, Samantha let her emotions fly without holding back. "How could you let this happen to my baby? How could you!? One minute I was in a business meeting – next I had to cut my business trip short and catch the first flight out of London! What happened? How did it happen?"

"We'd just returned from ballet class. I was preparing dinner and Lia was finishing up her homework. The lightbulb must've burned out. She got another one from the hall closet and tried to replace it herself and it exploded. When she screamed, I was there in seconds and the ziekenwagen (ambulance) arrived in no time. I've been praying her eyes will be okay, that she'll be okay."

"You pray in your sleep then, do you?" Samantha asked, without waiting for an answer. "The artsen (physicians) say she'll never see again," Samantha said with an unkind venom in her delivery.

M EANWHILE, LIA WAS IN a dream, flying with an angel. She had her arms around his neck, as she snuggled up against his chest. The movement of the wheelchair in the air rocker and comforted her.

Then her mind rolled over and she was looking down at a metal container from above. The container was sitting on the seat of a wheelchair with wings. It was being transported to where she did not know.

She held up her right hand and then here left, and with them she could see that there was an angel/boy trapped inside it. He had a kind face, with eyes bluer than the sky with flecks of gold which made them sparkle even though he was in the dark. His hair was, mostly blond other than some greying at the temples. But the strangest thing was a black streak down the middle. It made the boy appear older.

The angel/boy in the container riding on the seat of the wheelchair flew closer to the little girl in her dream. She touched the container, and when she did, she could feel and hear the heartbeat of the angel/boy inside. Not only that, but she could also read his thoughts and emotions.

Lia woke up and cried out, "Mother! Hannah! Come quickly!"

"I'm here, darling," her mother said, as she made her way back to her daughter's bedside.

Hannah wiped her eyes and re-entered the room.

"There is no time for you mother to place blame on Hannah. This was an accident. Besides, our help is needed. Please find me some paper and pencils - NOW."

"She's delirious!" Samantha exclaimed. She checked her daughter's forehead for a temperature. It seemed fine.

Hannah retrieved the items requested from her bag and placed them into Lia's hands.

Without hesitation, Lia began to draw. She scratched away at the paper, like an inspired artist. Samantha and Hannah looked on with curiosity.

The first picture she drew, was of a boy inside of a metal bullet shaped container. The container was resting in the seat of a wheelchair and the wheelchair had wings. Angel wings. Lia turned the page and drew a second picture of a boy/angel inside from all angles. From all sides. After the first picture, she drew many more maniacally, and then she threw them up into the air.

The pictures, like they were caught in a gust of wind – danced around the room, soaring up then, down, then all around. Like they were under a magical spell. One of the pictures chased the nanny, so she ran out of the room screaming.

Lia closed her fists tightly, then mumbled some inaudible words.

"Should I call the Doctor?" her hysterical mother asked. "My baby, oh no, my poor baby!"

Hannah returned, trembling as she looked on as Lia had drifted back to sleep.

The two women sat at the child's bedside. They watched her sleep peacefully until eventually they too drifted off to sleep.

Lia could not see with the hazel-coloured eyes she had been born with. They'd been replaced with eyes on the palms of her hands.

Her new palm placed eyes included every normal part an eye. Such as the pupil, the iris, the sclera, cornea, and tear duct. Each palm eye had an eyelid. The top began where the fingers ended. The bottom ended where the wrist began.

As to eyelashes, each finger had a hairline tattooed upon it. From the top of the eyelid to where the nail began, as did the thumb.

Which was a good thing, since no young girl would want fingers with hair growing upon them.

Especially not a little girl like Lia who hoped to one day to become a great ballet dancer.

CHAPTER TWO

W HEN SHE WOKE UP, the palms of her hands were very itchy. In fact, they were itchier than they'd ever been before. Which reminded her of something her grandmama once said. Grandmama said that when your right hand itched, it meant you'd be getting money and plenty of it. If your left hand itched, it meant you'd be losing money. She never said what would happen if both palms itched at the same time.

A flash of the angel/boy trapped in the container drew her back to reality. She opened her palms, preparing to scratch. Instead, was shocked to see herself reflected in them. She smiled, like she was posing for a selfie.

Still not one hundred percent certain if she was dreaming, she turned both palms away from her. Her intention was to take a panoramic view of the room.

It was decorated like she was swimming inside an aquarium. Clown fish and goldfish were busy chasing each other's tails. She continued moving her hands across the room until she found Hannah. Then she found her mother. She squealed in delight.

Lia's mother, Samantha jumped up as did Hannah.

"What is it baby?"

"Mommy? I can see you."

"Of course, you can my darling."

"Do you believe me?"

"Yes, of course I believe you. But tell me something, before, why did you draw a wheelchair with wings? Wheelchairs don't have wings."

She does not see my new eyes, Lia thought. "I love you, mommy, but some wheelchairs do have wings and some angels fly in wheelchairs with wings."

"Love you too baby," she replied. "What boy/angel? Did you have a dream?"

"There is a boy angel," Lia said.

"A boy/angel? Where baby?"

Lia opened the palms of her hands and thought about the angel boy. She thought so hard, she could see him, hear him, feel his presence in her mind. "The angel/boy is coming here to see me," she said.

"Here darling?" her mother asked, glancing in the direction of the nanny who shrugged her shoulders.

"Yes, the angel boy needs my help. He's coming to see me all the way from North America."

"When you drew the pictures," Hannah asked, "were you drawing from a memory of the angel/boy?"

"Or from a dream?" her mother asked.

"It started as a dream, but now I can see him when I'm awake, too."

"If you can see me baby, what am I wearing?"

"I can see you mommy, not with my old eyes. But with my new ones. You're wearing a red dress, with pearls around your neck."

An elderly patient passing by her room, stopped in his tracks when he saw a child, holding her palms open in front of her. *It's her*, he thought, and to confirm this he didn't have to wait long. For Lia, sensing another person's presence, turned her left palm in the direction of the door. The old man saw her palm blink, then stepped out of her sight.

"She's guessing," Hannah suggested, turning Lia's attention away from the doorway.

A nurse arrived and Lia, who'd never seen her before, said, "Hello, Nurse Vinke."

"Have we met before?" Nurse Heidi Vinke asked.

Lia giggled. "No, but I can read your nametag."

"She says she can see, with her new eyes," Lia's mother said.

"There, there," Nurse Vinke replied, tending to the mother instead of the little girl. The child didn't mind when Nurse Vinke took her mother outside to speak with her privately.

"It's normal for your daughter to use her imagination under the circumstances, she has lost her sight. She is a happy little thing, even though a terrible thing has happened to her."

Samantha nodded and the two returned to Lia.

"You must be tired child," Nurse Vinke said, taking the little girl's pulse.

"I'm not," Lia said. "I just woke up and I don't want to go back to sleep again. If I sleep now, I might miss him."

"Miss who?" Vinke asked, tucking the little girl in.

"Why, the boy/angel," Lia said. "He's getting closer now. Nearly here - and he needs my help. I can't wait to meet him. He's travelled a long, long way, just to see me."

"There, there, child," Vinke cooed. She pressed a needle filled with sleep inducing medicine into Lia's arm.

Lia protested, but then immediately fell asleep.

"Night, night, baby," her mother cooed.

T HE ELDERLY MAN RETURNED to his room and picked up the
phone. Then he demanded an outside line.

"She's here," he whispered into the phone. "I saw her for myself –
right here in the hospital down the hall from my room."

There was silence, then a click on the other end. The old man got into
bed. He turned on the television with the remote.

His favourite program: Now or Neverland (also known as Fear Factor)
was just starting. He wanted to see what those crazy fools would be
getting up to in this week's episode.

CHAPTER THREE

STILL CRAMPED INSIDE THE silver bullet, E-Z no longer felt so alone. For in his mind, he was talking with a little girl.

She'd come into his mind accompanied by a flash of light and a scream. She'd been injured. He watched as the angel Haniel helped her. He listened when Haniel sang a song to the little girl while she removed the glass.

What came next was unexpected. The angel Haniel drew lines upon the little girl's palm and fingers. Haniel gifted the child a new kind of sight. And palm eyes.

He knew at once that the little girl's fate was connected to his.

At first, although he could see her in his mind, he was unable to communicate with her. It was like he was watching a television program in his mind without the sound. Then, when the child dreamed, she came to him and placed her hands upon the bullet he was trapped in. Then he knew what she knew, and she knew what he knew, and they were linked.

The first words she had spoken to him were, "I don't like the dark."

E-Z had replied, "Don't be afraid. I am here. My name is E-Z. And what is your name?"

"My name is Cecilia," the child replied. "But my friends call me Lia. You may call me Lia. I am seven years old. How old are you?"

E-Z had thought the child was younger. "I'm thirteen," he said. "I'm from North America."

"I live in the Netherlands," Lia said.

Both were silent as Lia used her palm eyes to look at him inside the steel bullet.

"What are you doing in there?" she inquired.

E-Z thought before answering. He did not want to frighten the child, with the true story in that he had been kidnapped as a trial by an archangel. He wanted to tell her the truth, but he wasn't sure she could handle the truth since she was so young.

He said, "I'm not really certain why I was put in here, but I think it was, that I was put in here to meet you." He hesitated, scratched his head, and asked, "Do you know Eriel?"

Lia was flattered, that he was coming to see her but concerned he was being transported in such a way for her benefit. "I'm so sorry, if you are being forced against your will, travelling this way to meet me. Oh and no, that name is not known to me."

E-Z was very curious about Lia. Since she said she was Dutch, he was extremely impressed how excellent her English was.

"I felt you, but couldn't see you until the eyes, my new eyes grew. Before that, I could read your thoughts. Could you read mine? Oh, and thank you, about my English."

"I saw what happened to you, the accident. I'm deeply sorry you were hurt. I was unable to help you, because of this thing." He pounded his fists against the walls. He covered his ears, as the pounding noise reverberated. "When you dreamed, you were with me. Inside my head."

Lia closed her right fist, leaving the left one open and touching the exterior wall. Her palm blinked open and then closed, open and then closed. She said nothing but stared ahead like one who was in a trance.

E-Z decided at this time to tell her his story.

"My parents were killed in a car accident. And I lost the use of my legs."

He stopped there. Wondering how much he should tell her.

This hesitation made the decision for him.

She was sound asleep.

CHAPTER FOUR

BACK AT THE HOSPITAL, a new doctor was on duty. He looked at Lia's chart briefly. Seeing Cecelia was still sleeping he whispered to her mother.

"We need to take your daughter down to the second floor, for another scan."

"Is this urgent?" Lia's mother asked. "She's sleeping so peacefully; it would be a shame to wake her up."

The doctor whose nametag was covered by the collar of his medical jacket smiled. "No need to wake her up. We can slide her into the machine while she's sleeping. Some patients, especially the younger ones prefer it this way."

Samantha looked at her watch. "Sure thing, I'll go down with her."

"No need," the doctor said. "I have assistants coming along momentarily. Take advantage of the time to get yourself a sandwich or a cup of chamomile tea – my wife swears by the stuff. Helps her relax and to sleep."

"Thank you," Samantha said, as two attendants arrived. The two burly men dressed in street clothes lifted Lia from the bed and placed her onto a gurney with wheels. The doctor pulled a blanket from below the gurney and put it onto Lia. "We'll keep her warm and be back in no time at all. Don't forget about taking advantage of this time to treat yourself to a tea or coffee."

While Hannah slept on, Samantha watched the attendants and doctor as they pushed her daughter along the corridor. Now at the elevator waiting, she watched more closely. As the elevator doors closed, she meandered along the hallway ignoring a gut feeling which was nagging at her. She brushed it away, telling herself she was hungry and made her way to the cafeteria. It was very was busy. Mostly with staff members wearing scrubs.

As she prepared and sipped her tea, it occurred to her that no staff members wore street clothing.

"Excuse me," she said to one of the doctors. "What's on the second floor? Is that where x-rays and body scans are taken?"

He shook his head, "Second floor is the maternity ward."

Samantha rose from her chair, knocking over her hot tea and spilling it onto her lap as she did so. Helpers came from all directions when she screamed.

"My daughter!" she cried. "A doctor with two assistants just took my daughter Lia away on a gurney. They said they were taking her to the second floor for some tests. If the second floor is for maternity, why would they have taken her away?

Her outburst was attracting to much attention. So, the doctor she'd addressed in the first place coaxed her outside.

They returned to Lia's room. Samantha explained everything in more detail. Good thing she'd looked at her watch so she could tell them the exact time it had all happened.

"This is a serious matter," Doctor Brown said. "Leave it with me. We have security cameras all over the hospital. Perhaps you misheard about the second floor? Perhaps she on the seventh floor getting a scan right now as we speak. Leave it with me. Sit tight here and I'll be back to you as soon as possible."

Samantha sat down and explained everything to Hannah. They shared the tuna sandwich and tried hard not to worry.

W HILE LIA SLEPT ON, the man who wasn't really a doctor and the interns who were not interns left the building. They went to a waiting car. Left the gurney in the parking lot.

Doctor Brown called a meeting with the Administrator. Using Video Surveillance, they witnessed Lia's abduction. They alerted the police, giving a description of the vehicle. Unfortunately, the cameras did not pick up the license plate details.

"Let's wait a bit," Helen Mitchell, the Hospital Administrator said. She was retiring in just a few days. "Before we update the little girl's mother. We don't want to worry her."

"I can't do that," Doctor Brown said.

"The police might bring the child back in no time at all."

"I'm hoping you're right. Still, it's a worry. Hopefully, they don't get far."

The phone rang, it was the police. They put an all-points bulletin (APB) out on the little girl. They asked for a recent photo of her.

"They want a recent photo," Helen Mitchell said.

"The only way to get one is to ask her mother," Doctor Brown said.

Helen nodded, as Brown turned to leave.

"Tell them we'll fax it over asap."

"I'll send someone up from the trauma team," Helen said. Then to the police on the phone, "She blind and only seven-years-old. Why on earth would these three men go to such elaborate lengths to remove her from the hospital like this?"

"I can't say," the officer on the other end said.

CHAPTER FIVE

E-Z IMMEDIATELY KNEW SOMETHING wasn't right with his new friend Lia. She was meant to be sleeping in her hospital bed, but her bed was on the move. What the?

He considered waking her up, but what could she do even if he did? No, best she slept on – until he could find her and rescue her. As it was, she was busily dreaming of herself performing a ballet dance. He'd never paid much attention to ballet before, but it seemed to him that this little girl was talented. And she was dancing using the eyes in her hands as she moved across the stage.

E-Z transported himself in his mind to her location without much effort. There she was, fast asleep in the backseat of a moving vehicle. She looked so peaceful, because she was away in her mind doing something she loved – dancing.

He broadened his view, and he saw three heads. The one driving was of normal size and stature. Whereas the other two men looked like football players.

"Speed it up!" E-Z commanded his chair, but it had already done so.

How was he going to help her, when he was trapped inside of the silver bullet still? He needed to break it to smithereens – and sooner rather than later. Thus far, every effort to break it hadn't worked.

He wondered why the men had taken her. Did they know of her powers? How could they have known? Most hospitals had CCTV, could they have been watching her? It didn't make any sense though. She was a seven-year-old blind girl. What did they want from her?

As E-Z burned with speed across the sky, he couldn't help but wonder why they'd kidnapped her. Did they intend to demand a ransom?

In any case if that's what they were after it made more sense to him. Better than them knowing she was sighted. With special powers to boot. Still, his number one priority was to get out of the bullet.

He screamed. Like he's done many times before, "HELP!"

POP.

"Hello," Hadz said, while sitting upon E-Z's shoulder. "What the heck are you doing in here? This place is too small for you." Hadz rolled her eyes.

E-Z was more than a little excited to see Hadz. He grabbed the little creature and hugged her tightly to his chest.

"Uh, watch the wings," Hadz said.

E-Z let the creature go. "Thank you for coming and answering my call. I totally need you to help me figure out how to get out of this thing. I know you have been removed from my case, but there's a little girl named Lia and she's in danger and she needs me. You simply have got to help. I'm sure Eriel will understand."

"Oh, so you don't want to be in this thing then?" Hadz asked.

"No, I do not want to be in here. I want out, but how?"

"Just do it," Hadz said.

"I've tried everything. The sides won't budge. I summoned Eriel to help me, but he said I was on my own in this one."

"Ah, he wouldn't like that. I'm not supposed to help, but one thing I can say to you is: consider your surroundings."

"That's no help," E-Z said, trying not to totally lose his temper. "I asked the chair to take me to Uncle Sam. He'd for sure get me out of this thing. But the chair ignored my wishes. Now, a little girl is in trouble, and she needs my help. If I can't get out, then I can't help myself and if I can't help myself then I can't help her. Please. Tell me how to get out of here. Zap me out or something."

The creature shook her head then flew up to the top of the bullet. Touched the tip. "Consider physics. If you are inside of a bullet, which is what this thing resembles, then you must be discharged. Fired. Correct?"

E-Z considered his options. He could tell the chair to drop him, launching him toward the ground. The ground would break his fall. Would it break the bullet wide open? He decided it was worth the risk. "Okay," E-Z said, "I need to get the chair to drop me, right?"

The creature laughed. "You are funny, E-Z. If you dropped from this height, this thing would be embedded in the ground. That's providing it didn't explode upon impact. And with you in it." She laughed again. "Or you didn't die in the fall. If you died you couldn't save the little girl. Hey, what little girl are you talking about anyway?"

"Her name is Cecelia, Lia and she's in the Netherlands, not far from where we are now."

Hadz felt the tip of the container which E-Z had not seen, nor could he have reached. The creature pushed it. The cylinder released and popped open like a tulip. Hadz helped E-Z out of the bullet and soon he was sitting in his chair, holding the thing on his lap. E-Z's wings opened. It felt good to stretch them.

E-Z took off across the sky, carrying the cylinder which he dropped into the North Sea.

The trio, E-Z, the chair and Hadz flew at high speed and flew towards North Holland where the car was speeding along.

"Thanks," E-Z said.

"You're welcome," Hadz replied. "I'll stick around in case you need me."

"Awesome!"

CHAPTER SIX

E-Z WAS CATCHING UP to the car, which was now nearing Zaandam. He checked and Lia was still sleeping away in the backseat. She was no longer dreaming though, so he worried she might wake up soon.

His wheelchair changed course, sped up and zeroed in on the car, then hovered above it. The fake doctor who was driving, spotted the wheelchair in behind them in the side mirror.

"Wat is dat vliegende contraptie?" he asked. (Translation: What is that flying contraption?"

The two thugs turned their heads.

One said, "Ik weet het niet, maar versnel het!" (Translation: I don't know but speed it up!"

The second thug laughed then removed a gun from the dashboardkastje. (Translated: glove box.) He checked for bullets. Snapped it shut and clicked the catch off.

E-Z's wheelchair landed on the roof of the car with a clunk.

The driver braked hard, causing the wheelchair to slide forward. It slid down the windshield facing forwards then across the hood.

E-Z lifted off, hovered, and turned to face them.

"What the?" the driver shouted, as he lost control of the car, causing it to skid and zigzag.

E-Z and the wheelchair lifted off, backtracking, and grabbing a hold of the car's bumper causing it to come to a full stop.

Instantly, the passenger was thrown open and shots were fired.

In the backseat Lia snored away.

The thug with the gun rolled out the door, then on his knees prepared to fire a shot at E-Z.

Hadz came out of nowhere and knocked the gun out of the thug's hand. She then tied his hands behind his back and his feet behind his back like he was a calf at a rodeo.

The second thug went straight for E-Z, who lassoed him with his belt. The thug fell over, so he could easily wrap the belt around his legs.

The guy tried to hop away but didn't get far. Now that he was stopped, they went for the doctor using the chair's caging mechanism. The doctor was caught and immobilized.

Lia slept through it all, even while Hadz lifted her out of the vehicle and carried to to safety.

E-Z placed the three men side by side in the backseat of the car.

"Who do you work for?" he demanded.

Hadz flew over, "They don't understand English." To the men she translated E-Z's question. After the fake doctor answered, Hadz translated. "He says they don't know who they are working for."

"That's ridiculous. They kidnapped a child from the hospital. Ask them where they were taking her then? And how did they find out about her?"

Hadz translated. The fake doctor again answered with, "We were told to take her to the dock, and someone would be waiting for her there. That's all we know."

E-Z didn't believe them, but Hadz confirmed they were indeed telling the truth. "What do you want to do with them?" she asked.

"Can you wipe their minds? And the minds of those they are connected to, These three are cogs in the machine. We want to wipe the mind of the person at the docks. So, they all forget about her – forever."

"Done," she said.

"Wow, you're fast!"

E-Z and Hadz in the chair made their way back to the hospital, just as Lia began to stir awake. She moved her head, felt the wind blowing her hair and snuggled into E-Z's chest. She opened her right palm and looked at her friend, the boy/angel. She laughed and hugged him tightly. When she noticed the little fairy-like creature on E-Z's shoulder, she used her palm eyes to look at her.

"You're so small and cute," she said.

"Pleased to me you," Hadz said. "And thank you."

They flew toward the hospital.

"You are safe now," E-Z said.

"And you're not in that thing anymore, "Lia said.

"Hadz helped me to get out," E-Z said, flapping his wings.

"Where did you get those?" Lia asked. "Can I have some?"

E-Z smiled. He wasn't sure how much he should tell her. He worried what Eriel would say if he revealed too much. "I got them after my parents died."

"But why?" little Lia inquired.

"I started rescuing people," E-Z said.

"You mean, I'm not the first person you've rescued?"

"No, you're not."

Hadz cleared her throat, which was a signal to E-Z to stop talking.

They flew on in silence. The little girl hugging E-Z's chest. The wheelchair knowing where it needed to go. Hadz feeling needed once again.

E-Z was lost in his thoughts. He wondered if rescuing Lia had been the main trial. Or if getting out of the bullet had completed the task. Maybe it was two for one! How many would that have been then? He had to write them down to keep track. That's what he had been doing in his journal, but as of late he'd not had much time to record things.

"I can hear you thinking," Lia said. She had both of her palms open. She was watching E-Z's outside while listening to what he was thinking inside. "I want to know more about these trials. And I want to know why I can see with my hands instead of my eyes. Do you think this Eriel will know?"

POP

Hadz didn't wait around for the answer.

"The hospital is below," E-Z said.

The chair descended slowly, and they went inside the hospital. E-Z and the chair's wings disappeared. He pushed along the corridor and found Lia's room. Her mother was waiting there.

"Arrest this boy," Lia's mother screamed.

E-Z was flabbergasted. Why would she want him to be arrested? He'd just saved her daughter.

"But Mommy," Lia began.

The police came in. They reached behind E-Z and put his hands into cuffs.

Before they closed them, Lia screamed. Then she opened the palms of her hands and held them out in front of her. From her palm eyes a blinding white light came forth causing everyone in the room except for she and E-Z to stop in time. Little Lia stopped time.

"Cool! How did you do that?" E-Z exclaimed as the handcuffs dropped onto the floor with a clunk.

"I, I don't know. I wanted to protect you. To save you." She stopped, listened. "Someone is coming, you've got to get out of here. I can feel someone else is coming, and you must be gone."

"Someone?" E-Z asked. "Do you know who?"

"I don't know. All I know is, someone else is coming, and you need to go - immediately."

"Will you be, okay? Are they going to hurt you?"

"I'll be fine – they are coming for you – not me. Get out of here, now."

"When will I see you again?" E-Z asked, as he smashed the hospital window and flew out and waited for her to answer.

"You shall always see me, E-Z. We are interlinked. We are friends. You get out of here and I'll manage the rest." She blew him a kiss.

Lia got into bed, pulled the covers up to her neck and pretended she was sound asleep before she set the world to moving once again.

"What happened?" her mother asked.

Everything was well again. Lia was in bed unharmed.

The world continued as it had done before while E-Z winged his way back home again.

"Thanks, Hadz for helping," E-Z said even though she had gone. Somehow, he knew that wherever she was, she could hear him.

CHAPTER SEVEN

As E-Z flew across the sky, he realized he was starving. Below him was Big Ben. He decided to land and get himself some English Fish and Chips.

As the chair descended, he noticed a white van moving quickly down the road. It was parallel to a school. He saw parents in vehicles and on foot waiting to collect their children.

As the van turned the corner, it picked up speed.

His wheelchair lurched forward, falling in behind the vehicle. The driving was getting more reckless, as it neared the school. Children started coming out.

E-Z grabbed onto the back of the van. Using all his strength, he pulled it to a full stop with a squeal.

The driver stepped on the gas, trying to pull away. He had zero luck. They couldn't see what or who was holding them back.

E-Z broke the lock on the trunk, reached inside and pulled out the jumper cables. The chair lurched forwards and landed on the roof of the vehicle. E-Z used the jumper cables to tie up the cab doors. The driver couldn't get out.

The sounds of sirens filled the air.

E-Z took flight, and noticing several people were taking his picture on their phones flew higher and higher.

His stomach grumbled and he remembered the fish and chips. Having no British currency, he couldn't pay for them anyway, so he made his way home.

Thinking about his Uncle wondering where he was, he thought he'd leave a message and started to do so, "I'm on the way home."

Click.

"Where are you?" Uncle Sam asked.

E-Z was pleased it wasn't a message!

"I'm just flying over Britain. It's a pleasant day for flying, don't you think?"

"What? How?"

"It's a long story, I'll explain when I'm back."

"Are you in a plane?"

"Nope, it's just me and my chair."

Below, E-Z could see people taking photos of him. When he spotted a local carrier 747 coming his way, he realized he was in trouble. Before he had the chance to fly higher cameras were taking photos and posting them all over social media.

"Sorry Eriel," he said, taking himself up higher. "You know the saying any publicity is good publicity? Well..." E-Z laughed. If Eriel could see him every day and every hour, they why did he have to summon him for help? Something didn't quite add up. Not I the archangels wanted him to complete the trials.

A chill went through him as the sky changed as black clouds swirled and pulsed all around him. He flew on, trying to pick up the pace, but then the lightning bolts started, and he needed to dodge them. Then he remembered the plane. He could see that it was making a successful landing, and the people were unharmed. He continued towards home.

After the storm, the stars came out. His chair kept flapping its wings while E-Z took a nap.

"E-Z?" Lia said in his head. "Are you there?"

He jerked awake, forgot he was in the chair and fell out. He began to fall, but his wings kicked in and soon he was back in the chair again.

"Is everything okay, little one?" he asked.

"Yes. They think it was all a dream, me talking to you. Drawing pictures of you. Mommy knows the truth, but she won't face up to it."

"Oh, does that worry you?"

"No. My powers are increasing. I can feel them, and I know that something is coming. Something which you will need my help with. I'll be going home soon. I'm going to ask Mommy if we can visit you. Soon."

"What? Your Mom should call my Uncle Sam and they can chat?"

"Yes, that's a clever idea. Mom has seen the photos, and she has met you, but she doesn't remember. It's like her mind was cleaned or her memories of you are sleeping."

"Are you sure this is the right thing to do?"

"I'm sure. I need to be where you are. I need to help you."

E-Z's mind went blank. Lia was gone.

The teenager thought about Lia, coming to North America. She was a little girl, sighted with her hands, yes, but how could she help him? She had helped him escape, but he was confused about her involvement. He did not want to put her in danger. He called out to Eriel again. He evoked the chant, but nothing happened.

He took in the scenery, taking his mind of the little girl for a moment. He was nearly home now. Thank goodness his chair was modded and he could travel F-A-S-T!

CHAPTER EIGHT

Just ahead, E-Z spotted the coast. He sighed in relief until he noticed a large bird headed straight for him. As it neared, he realized it was a swan. But not your normal sized swan. It was huge and so was its wingspan which he estimated for over one hundred and fifty inches. It was the same swan who had spoken to him before. And not only that, but he also noticed a bright red-light flickering on the bird's shoulder.

The swan veered and then landed heavily on his shoulders. It had hitched a ride.

"Well, hello there," E-Z said, glancing up at the beautiful creature as it steadied itself.

"Hoo-hoo," the swan said. Then it shook its head, opened its beak, and said, "Hello E-Z."

"I believe I owe you my thanks," he said.

"Oh, you're very welcome. And I hope you don't mind that I hitched a ride," the swan said, ruffling its feathers.

"Uh, no problem," E-Z replied.

"This is my mentor Ariel," the swan said.

WHOOPEE

An angel replaced the red light.

"Hello," she said, sitting on E-Z's knee.

"Uh, nice to meet you," he said.

"How can I be of service?" he asked.

"I'm hoping that you, and my friend the swan here will be able to form a partnership."

"How so?" he asked.

"My protégé has been through a lot. He can fill you in on the details when he feels ready, but for now I need you to help him by allowing him to help you with the trials. You can use some help, yes?"

"From my understanding," he said directed at Ariel. Then to the swan, "nothing against you, mate." Now to Ariel, "is that no one can help me in my trials. That came directly from Eriel and Ophaniel."

"I've cleared it with them. So, if that's your only objection," she paused then

WHOOPEE

and she was gone.

After that E-Z and the swan continued across the Atlantic Ocean and on into North America. As he always wanted to see the Grand Canyon. He'd have to see it at another time. The swan snored and snuggled in against E-Z's neck.

E-Z reached into his pocket and pulled out his phone. He took a selfie with the swan. He kept his phone in his hand, planning to record the swan the next time it spoke. He needed proof that he wasn't losing his mind.

Sometime later, E-Z zeroed in on his house. It was a school day, but he was way too tired to go. When the chair began its descent, the swan woke up. "Are we there yet?"

"Yes, we're at my home," E-Z said, pushing the record button on his phone. "Anywhere you'd like me to drop you off?"

"No thank you. I'm to stay with you," the swan said, as it lengthened its neck to have a look at the house he would be staying at. "You and I, we need to talk."

E-Z pressed play but it was dead air. The swan couldn't be recorded. Strange.

They landed at the front door. E-Z put his key into the lock but before he could open it Uncle Sam was there. He gave his nephew a big hug and said, "Welcome home." He scratched his chin and looked a little worried when he saw E-Z's companion, an exceptionally large swan.

"Glad to be back," E-Z said, making his way inside.

The swan followed with its webbed feet padding along behind him.

"And who's your, uh, feathered friend?" Uncle Sam asked.

E-Z realized he didn't even know the swan's name.

The swan said, "Alfred, my name is Alfred."

E-Z made a formal introduction.

The swan then padded off down the hall, into E-Z's room and it flew up onto his bed to take a well-earned nap.

E-Z went into the kitchen with Uncle Sam on his wheels.

"What on earth is that swan doing here?" He paused, took some milk out of the fridge. He poured his nephew a glass full. "It can't stay here. We'd have to put it into the bathtub. That if it fits. He's the biggest swan I've ever seen. Where did you find it and why did you bring it here?"

E-Z gulped back his milk. He wiped away his milk moustache. "I didn't find it, it found me. And it can talk. It, he, was there when I saved that little girl and when I saved that plane. He says we need to talk."

Uncle Sam without replying walked down the hall. E-Z followed closely behind without speaking.

"Speak!" Uncle Sam demanded.

Alfred the swan opened its eyes, yawned, and then went back to sleep again without even emitting a sound.

"I said, speak," Uncle Sam said, trying again.

Alfred the swan opened his beak and snorted.

"It's okay, Alfred," E-Z said. "It's my Uncle Sam."

"He can't understand me. And I don't think he ever will be able to. I'm here for you and for you only," said Alfred the swan. He snorted, then snuggled into the duvet and drifted off to sleep once again.

Uncle Sam looked on, while the swan had been animated and looking intently at E-Z.

He and Uncle Sam closed the door on their way out and went back into the kitchen to talk.

E-Z was so tired, he could hardly keep his eyes open.

"Can't this wait until morning," he asked.

Sam shook his head.

"Okay, here goes. First, I hit a baseball out of the park. And I ran or wheeled around the bases. Then, I was trapped inside of a bullet-shaped container with no way out. Then I could speak with a little girl in The Netherlands. I went there to rescue her. Her name is Lia, and her mother will be calling you. I stopped a vehicle from harming kids, in London, England. Then I met Alfred the trumpeter swan. And now you're up to speed – can I please go to bed?"

"What am I supposed to say when she calls?" Sam inquired. "We don't even know these people, but we're supposed to let them stay here in the house with us. Us and Alfred the swan?"

"Yes, please go along with it. There is a plan at work here and I don't know all the details yet. Lia has powers, eyes in the palms of her hands and she can read my thoughts and stop time. Alfred the swan also has powers, he can read my mind and he can talk. I think we three are linked in some way, perhaps because of the trials. I don't know. Anything can happen with Eriel spying on me 24-7," E-Z said.

Coming along the corridor, they heard the slapping of the swan's feet as it waddled along. "I'm too hungry to sleep," Alfred the swan said.

"What kind of things do you eat?"

"Corn is good, or you can let me out back and I'll get myself some grass."

"Do we have any corn?" E-Z asked.

"Only frozen," Uncle Sam said. "But I can run the kernels under warm water, and they'll be ready in a jiff."

"Tell him thank you," Alfred the swan said. "That is very kind of him."

Uncle Sam put the corn onto a plate and Alfred ate what was offered. He was still hungry though and he needed to go to empty his bladder, so he asked to go outside after all. While he was out, he would partake of the lawn.

E-Z and Uncle Sam watched the swan for a few seconds.

"I hope the neighbor's chihuahua doesn't pop round for a visit," Uncle Sam said. "That swan is so big it'll scare the living daylights out of him."

E-Z laughed. "Imagine what it would do, if the dog could understand it like I can?"

Alfred the swan made himself at home. He felt certain he would be happy here.

CHAPTER NINE

L ATER, ALFRED THE SWAN asked to speak with E-Z privately.

"You can say whatever here," E-Z said. "Uncle Sam doesn't understand you, remember?"

"Yes, I know. But it's a matter of manners. One does not speak to a person when another is present, especially when a guest in another's home. It would be, well, rather rude. In fact, very rude."

E-Z only now realized that Alfred the swan spoke with a British Accent.

"Might I be excused?" E-Z asked.

Uncle Sam nodded and E-Z went into his room with Alfred the swan following.

"Okay," E-Z said. "Tell me why Ariel sent you here and what exactly it is you intend to do to help me?"

Now that E-Z was in his bed, the swan swanned around as he kneaded into the duvet, trying to get comfy.

"You can sleep at the bottom of the bed," E-Z said, tossing a pillow there.

"Thank you," Alfred the swan said. He waddled onto the pillow and pummeled it with his webbed feet until it was comfy. Then squatted down.

"Now, let's begin," Alfred said.

E-Z, now in his pajamas listened as Alfred told his story.

"I was a man once."

E-Z gasped.

"Best not to interrupt until I'm finished," the swan scolded. "Otherwise, my tale will go on and on and neither of us will get any sleep."

"Sorry," E-Z said.

The swan continued. "I lived with my wife and two children. We were incredibly happy, until a storm blew through and tore down our house and killed them all. I survived but without them did not want to. Then an angel came to me, Ariel who you met, and she told me I could see them all once again, if I agreed to help others. I enjoy helping others and doing so would give me purpose. Besides, I had no other options and so I agreed."

"You have trials?" E-Z asked. He had wrongly assumed Alfred's tale had been completed.

"My story has not ended yet," Alfred the swan said, rather crossly. He then continued. "That's the crux of my story. I do not have trials, because I am not an angel in training. My wings are not like your wings. I am a swan, albeit a larger than usual swan. My breed's name is the Cygnus Falconeri, which is also known as the giant swan. My species became extinct a long time ago. My purpose was undefined. I was stuck in the betwixt and the between, drifting through time because I made a mistake. But I don't want to talk about that now. When I saw you save that little girl, I called Ariel and asked if I could be of service to you. She scolded me for escaping and I was sent back to the betwixt and the between. I escaped from there again and helped you with the plane and Ariel asked Ophaniel to give me another chance. Now I have a purpose - to help you."

"And Ophaniel, agreed? But what about Eriel?"

"They didn't at first. That was because Hadz and Reiki reported me for helping you by summoning my bird friends. When I heard that they were sent to the mines, and escaped again, Ariel put my case forward and Ophaniel agreed. I don't know about Eriel. Is he your mentor?"

"Yes, he took over for Hadz and Reiki. They popped in and out, whereas he says he can always see where I am and what I'm doing."

"That sounds like overkill. Still, I'd like to meet him one day. For now, we're a team. I can help you, so that one day, I too, will be with my family again. So, where you go E-Z, go I."

E-Z rested his head on his pillow and closed his eyes. He felt grateful for any help. After all the swan had helped him in the past with the plane.

"I won't get in your way," Alfred the swan said. "I know, you are thinking we are an illogical pair and when Lia arrives, we shall be an even more illogical trio but..."

"Wait," E-Z said. "You know about Lia? How?"

"Oh yes, I know all about you and I know all about her and I also know more. That the three of us are linked. Predestined to work together." He stretched his jaws, which looked like he was trying to yawn. "I'm too tired to talk anymore tonight." Before long Alfred, the swan was snoring away.

E-Z went over everything he knew in his mind about swans. Which wasn't much. In the morning, he'd do some research on Alfred's species.

He wondered how PJ and Arden were going to feel about Alfred. Did he need to introduce them or could Alfred be a secret?

He fluffed up his pillow with his fists and prepared to go to sleep.

It woke Alfred up, and he was cranky about it.

"Do you have to do that?" Alfred asked.

"Sorry," E-Z said.

CHAPTER TEN

T HE NEXT MORNING, E-Z awoke to the sound of Uncle Sam pounding on his door. "Wake up E-Z! PJ and Arden are already on the way to take you to school."

E-Z yawned and stretched. He dressed then maneuvered himself into his chair. Since Alfred was still asleep, he'd sneak out and see him after school.

"You can't go anywhere without me!" Alfred said. He shook his feathers all over and then jumped down onto the floor.

"You can't go with me to school. Pets aren't allowed."

"E-Z, come on lad!" Uncle Sam shouted from the kitchen. "Otherwise, you'll miss breakfast."

E-Z's stomach growled as the smell of toast wafted in his direction. "Coming!"

With no time to argue, E-Z opened the door. He made his way into the kitchen just as Arden and PJ arrived. A honk outside let him know they were there.

"Alright, alright!" E-Z called out as he grabbed a piece of toast. He made his way along the corridor with his new web-footed companion bringing up the rear behind him.

PJ got out of the car to help E-Z in and secured his wheelchair in the trunk. As he was closing it, he spotted Alfred attempting to get into the vehicle.

"Uh, that thing can't get in the car," PJ shouted.

Arden rolled down the window.

"What the heck is that? Did I miss a memo saying we were having *Show and Tell* today?" He sniggered.

"Is that a swan?" Mrs. Handle PJ's mother inquired.

"Or is this thing President of your fan club?" PJ asked with a smirk.

Once inside the car, E-Z answered. "We're too old for show and tell," he laughed. "The swan is my project. An experiment, like a seeing eye dog for a blind person. He is my wheelchair companion." He buckled Alfred in the seat belt.

PJ went to sit in the front beside his mother.

Alfred the swan said, "Aren't you going to introduce me?"

Mrs. Handle pulled the car out and they made their way to school.

"Alfred," E-Z glanced at his friends, "meet Mrs. Handle. And my two best friends PJ and Arden. Everyone, this is Alfred, the trumpeter swan." E-Z crossed his arms.

Alfred said, "Hoo-hoo." To E-Z he said, "I'm incredibly pleased to meet you. You can translate for me."

"How do you know his name?" PJ asked.

"You're not turning into, what was his name, the guy who could talk to animals now are you E-Z? Please tell me you're not. Although, it could turn into a real cash cow. We could market your talent. Ask for questions, and post answers on our own YouTube Channel. We could call it E-Z Dickens the Swan Whisperer."

"Excellent idea!" PJ said as his mother stopped at a crosswalk. "A few years ago, we probably would have made millions online. Nowadays making cash online is rough. They've really clamped down."

"Don't be rude," Mrs. Handle said, as she drove on.

"The person he is referring to is Doctor Dolittle," Alfred offered. "It was a twelve-book series of novels written by Hugh Lofting. The first book was published in 1920, and the others followed, right up until 1952. Hugh Lofting died in 1947. He was British also. A Berkshire man born and bred."

"I know who they mean," E-Z said to Alfred. "And no, I'm not."

Arden said, "I hope your swan companion doesn't steal all the girls from us today. You know how girls love feathery things."

Mrs. Handle cleared her throat.

"I was quite a lady killer, in my day," Alfred said, followed by another, "Hoo-hoo!" which he directed at PJ and Arden.

PJ said, "Your companion swan really cracks me up."

Arden asked, "What bird movie won an Oscar?"

PJ replied, "Lord of the Wings."

Arden asked, "Where do birds invest their money?"

PJ replied, "In the stork market!"

"Your friends are easily amused," Alfred said. "They are two plonkers, cut from the same cloth. I can see why you like them. I like Mrs. Handle. She's quiet and an excellent driver."

E-Z laughed.

"Glad you are enjoying the morning humour," PJ said.

"I'm not really," Alfred said. "Besides you two are real plonkers."

Arden and PJ did a double take.

E-Z also did a double take at their double takes. "What?"

"Didn't you hear that?" the two said in unison. "The swan can talk – and with a British accent. Oh man, the girls are really going to love him."

Mrs. Handle shook her head. "Don't play silly beggars you two!"

E-Z looked at Alfred the swan who seemed confused.

Alfred tried a joke of his own to see if they could really understand him. "Why do hummingbirds hum?" he asked.

The three boys looked on, it was clear both Arden and PJ could now understand him.

Alfred said the punchline, "Because they don't know the words, of course."

PJ and Arden laughed, sort of, but they were mostly freaked out.

"How come they can understand you too now?" E-Z asked. "First, they couldn't now they can. I thought you said it was only me. And why couldn't Uncle Sam understand you?"

Now that they could understand him, Alfred felt self-conscious. He whispered to E-Z, "I honestly don't know. Unless, what I'm here for has something to do with them too."

"And doesn't include Uncle Sam? Or Mrs. Handle?"

"Perhaps not," Alfred replied.

"And where, did you find this talking swan?" Arden asked.

"And why are you bringing him to school?" PJ asked.

Mrs. Handle huffed. "You are all being very silly. E-Z says he's a companion swan. He can't talk."

"First of all, he's not just a swan he's a Cygnus Falconeri. Also known as a giant swan and a species which has been extinct for centuries."

"I haven't seen many swans in real life," Arden said. "The ones I've seen on the nature channel didn't seem as big as he is though. His feet are huge! And what happens if he has to, you know, go to the toilet?"

"The average giant swan had a bill to tail length between 190-210 centimeters," Alfred offered. "And if I do, I'll use the grass – the sports field should give me ample space to feed and do my business if and when it is necessary."

"You mean you eat the grass and then you go on the grass?" PJ said.

"Eww!" Arden said.

They were awfully close to school now, so E-Z explained. "I can't give you details because I don't really know them. All I know for sure is that Alfred is here to help me, and you'll be seeing a lot of him."

"I don't think they are going to let him in the school," Arden said.

"It won't be a problem, since I'm your companion," Alfred said.

PJ, Arden, and Alfred laughed as the car came to a stop outside the school.

"Call me if you want me to collect you after school," Mrs. Handle said.

"Thanks," the replied.

After E-Z's chair was taken out of the trunk, Mrs. Handle pulled away from the curb.

His friends helped him into it, whereas Alfred flew up and sat on his shoulder. They made their way toward the front of the school where Principal Pearson was ushing students inside.

"Good morning boys," he said with a huge smile on his face. Until he noticed Alfred the swan. "What is that thing?" he asked.

"He's a companion swan," E-Z said.

"A Cygnus Falconerie, to be exact," Arden said.

"He's with us," PJ said.

Principal Pearson crossed his arms. "That thing, the Cygnus whatchamacallit is not coming in here!"

Alfred said, "It's okay E-Z. Let's not cause a scene. I'll be here when your classes end. See you later." Alfred flew up and landed on the roof of the building. He took in the view before flying down onto the football field. There was plenty of grass to munch on. When he was full, he'd find a shady spot under a tree and take a nap.

Principal Pearson shook his head, then held the door for E-Z and his friends. Inside the five-minute warning bell sounded.

This school day was uneventful for E-Z and his friends.

There was still no word from Eriel on any new trials.

CHAPTER ELEVEN

ALFRED SETTLED INTO HIS new routine. The kids at school got to know him – although only E-Z and his friends knew he could talk.

On this day, outside the school Alfred was waiting for E-Z and he asked, "Can we talk?"

E-Z looked around; he still didn't want the other students to overhear him talking to a swan. He whispered, "Uh, can this wait until we get home?"

"Oh, I see," Alfred said. "You still feel self-conscious when we're chatting. Which is understandable, but the kids love me here. They line up to pet me, to feed me. Besides, won't Uncle Sam be home? I need to talk to you alone."

"Since he can't understand you still, you are talking to me alone even when we're at home."

"But this is a matter of some concern and it's rather time sensitive," Alfred said.

PJ pulled up to the curb beside them. Arden asked if they wanted a ride home.

"Uh, guys. Sorry but I'm going to walk home with Alfred today. He has some vital information to impart to me."

PJ and Arden shook their heads. Arden said, "We expected to get thrown over one day for a girl – not a bird." He sniggered.

"And what about the game?" Arden asked.

"Today's today and the game isn't until tomorrow. Sorry guys." E-Z picked up the pace. The car crawled along beside him, then sped away with a squeal of the tires.

"Plonkers," Alfred said.

"They mean well. Now what's so important?"

"Have you heard anything from Lia lately? I'm worried about her." Alfred waddled along beside E-Z, nipping the head off a dandelion as he went.

"Why are you worrying? No news is good news, isn't it?"

"Well actually, I have heard from her and there has been a, uh, well, a perplexing new development."

E-Z stopped. "Tell me more."

"Keep walking," Alfred said, now nipping the head off a daisy. "Lia and her mother are already on the way here. They should be arriving sometime tomorrow."

"What the big hurry? I mean, yes, that is a surprise. We knew they would come soon. What's perplexing about that?"

"That's not the perplexing part."

"Stop stalling and spit it out!"

"Lia is no longer seven years old – she's now ten years old."

"What? That's impossible."

"Do you think she would lie?"

"No, I don't think she'd lie but – that makes absolutely no sense. People don't grow from seven to ten in a matter of weeks."

"She said she went to sleep. Next morning, she entered the kitchen for breakfast and her Nanny started screaming. That's how she discovered she'd aged three years overnight."

"Whoa!" E-Z exclaimed.

"And there's more."

"More. I can't imagine anything more."

"She was able to convince her mother there was no need for her to remain here for the entire visit. She's a busy businesswoman. It took quite a lot of persuading. Lia said she'd be better off given Sam's experience with you and the trials. Her mother agreed, under a few conditions."

"Such as?"

"That she likes Uncle Sam."

"Everybody likes Uncle Sam."

"Also, that you explain to her how her daughter could have aged like that overnight."

"And how exactly am I meant to do that?"

"To be honest," Alfred said, "I have no idea. That's why I wanted to talk to you alone. I mean, Uncle Sam knows that Lia is coming, right?"

E-Z nodded, "I guess so if they're on the way."

"But he expects a seven-year-old little girl, when a ten-year-old is going to show up on his doorstep."

E-Z stopped again. Uncle Sam. He hadn't even thought about Uncle Sam having to deal with a ten-year-old girl. "I'm not sure I ever mentioned Lia's age to him!"

Alfred rabbited on. "I've heard of humans aging quickly. There's a disease called Progeria. It's a genetic condition, quite rare and quite deadly. Most kids don't live past thirteen and Lia is already ten, so we need to figure this out."

"How is that thing you said,"

"Progeria."

"Yes, Progeria, how is it contracted?" E-Z asked.

"My understanding is it happens during the first couple of years. And the kids are usually disfigured."

"Lia is disfigured, because of the glass, not a disease. Is there a cure?"

"No cure. But E-Z, there's something else. It has something to do with the eyes in her hands. They are new and the disease is new. Too much of a coincidence don't you think?"

E-Z considered this and decided Alfred was right. It was too much of a coincidence. But what was he going to do about it? Should he call Eriel? "Do you know Eriel?"

Alfred slowed his pace and so did E-Z. They were nearly home and needed to talk this out before they met up with Uncle Sam. "Yes, I've heard of him. But as you know Eriel is not my angel. You met my mentor Ariel, and she is the angel of nature, hence me being in the condition of a rare swan. She may be able to help, but we'll have to wait for her next appearance to do so."

"You mean, you can't summon her?"

Alfred nodded. "Are you able to summon Eriel at will?"

E-Z laughed. "Not exactly at will, but he is reachable. Although, he's a pain in the you know what about it and doesn't like to be called upon or summoned." E-Z thought quietly and so did Alfred. Their house was in sight now and Uncle Sam was home as his car was parked in the driveway. "I think we should wait and see what happens with L ia."

"Agreed," Alfred said, as he stepped off the path and pulled some grass out of the ground and chewed on it. E-Z watched. "I prefer not to eat too much grass; I mean lawn grass. It's what I eat all day when you're at school – other than the few flowers I can find. Right now, I feel like having some of the wet stuff, growing underwater. It's fresher and juicer."

"I totally get that" E-Z said. "I like to eat salad when it's fresh and crunchy. I don't like it so much when it comes in bags and the only way to get it down is to drench it in salad dressing."

"I do miss human food."

"What do you miss the most?"

"Cheeseburgers and fries, without a doubt. Oh, and ketchup. How I used to love that thick, red gooey goes on everything sauce."

"Maybe it wouldn't be so bad, on grass?" E-Z laughed, but Alfred was thinking about it.

"I'd be willing to give it a go."

"Let's put it on your bucket list," E-Z said.

"What's a bucket list?" Alfred asked.

CHAPTER TWELVE

E-Z contemplated Alfred's question. Alfred didn't know what a bucket list was...and the phrase was coined in 2007. In the Nicholson/Freeman movie of the same name. He explained without going into too much detail.

"That's a really interesting idea," Alfred said, fluffing up his feathers. "But what's the point of keeping a bucket list? Surely, you'd remember anything you really wanted to do?"

"You know Alfred, I'm not exactly sure. I guess it might be something to do with age. Growing old and losing memory."

"Makes sense."

They continued along on their journey and arrived home. When E-Z wheeled himself up the ramp, Alfred hopped on. The swan flapped his wings to help with the upgoing momentum. At the top, as E-Z opened the door, they heard an unfamiliar voice.

"Oh no, they're already here!" Alfred said.

"You could have warned me!" E-Z replied, stowing his bag on a hook on the way into the living room.

"Obviously, I would have, had I known!"

Lia stood.

To E-Z ten-year-old Lia looked remarkably different, until she held up her open palms.

Lia squealed and ran to him and gave him a big hug. Then she hugged Alfred and said she was incredibly happy to finally meet him.

Lia's Mom Samantha was also standing, watching her daughter embrace the boy who had saved her life. The angel/boy in the wheelchair. Her daughter had mentioned Alfred, but not that he was a giant swan.

Uncle Sam stood and said, "Oh, E-Z! Thank goodness you're home!" He moved nearer to his nephew. Then awkwardly suggested they go into the kitchen to get refreshments.

"We're fine," Samantha said.

Sam insisted they go into the kitchen anyway.

"Uh," E-Z stammered. "I'd like a drink."

Sam sighed.

"Don't go to any trouble for us," Samantha said.

"It's no trouble at all," Sam said, pushing E-Z's chair toward the living room exit.

"Lia, you are very beautiful," Alfred said, bowing his head so she could pat him.

"Thank you," Lia said with a blush. She glanced in E-Z's direction as they left the room, but he didn't notice as his eyes were on his uncle.

Once they were in the kitchen Sam parked his nephew. He opened the fridge and closed it again. He went to the cupboard, opened the door, and closed it again.

"What's wrong?" E-Z asked.

"I, I didn't expect them so soon and what do people from the Netherlands eat and drink anyway? I don't think I have anything suitable in the house. Should I go out and get something special?"

"They are people just like us, I'm sure they'll try whatever you have. Don't overthink it."

"Help me out here, kiddo. What kind of things should we serve? Cheese and crackers? Something hot, grilled cheese sandwiches? We have water, and juice and soft drinks."

"Okay, let's do the cheese and crackers thing for now. See how we go with that. And a tray of assorted beverages."

Sam sighed and put it all together on a tray. "Oh, napkins!" he said, taking out a stack of them from the drawer.

"All set?" E-Z asked.

"Thanks, kiddo," Sam said, as he picked up the tray full of food and drinks. He made his way into the living room with his nephew following along behind him. Sam set everything onto the table then jumped up and said, "Side plates!" and left the room, returning shortly thereafter with the said items.

E-Z glanced in Lia's direction when he sipped his drink. He could still see her as a little girl, even though she wasn't one anymore. Her hair was longer.

Lia's Mom looked even more uncomfortable than Uncle Sam did. She fiddled with a cracker but did not bite into it. She moved the glass of drink back and forwards but did not drink from it. She glanced in Uncle Sam's direction every now and again, but not for long. Then sighed very loudly and went back to fiddling with her food.

"How was your flight?" E-Z asked.

"It was easy-peasy compared to flying with you," Lia said. She laughed and the soft drink nearly came out of her nose. Soon they were all laughing and feeling more at ease.

Alfred chatted freely, knowing that only Lia and E-Z could understand him. "Now we are together, *The Three*. As it was meant to be."

Lia and E-Z exchanged glances.

Alfred continued. "I keep wondering why we were brought together. E-Z you can save people and you're super-duper strong, plus you can fly and so can your chair. Lia your powers are in your sight. You can read thoughts. From what E-Z has told me you have the powers of light and can stop time.

"I, I can travel, fly in the sky and I can sometimes tell when things are going to happen before they happen. I can also read minds, not all the time. Also, most people love swans. Some say we are angelic. There are even those who believe swans have the power to transform people into angels. I don't know if that is true. I, myself, can help all living, breathing things to heal themselves."

The last part was new to E-Z. He wanted to know more.

Alfred volunteered, "Surrendering is the first step."

E-Z and Lia were lost in thoughts regarding Alfred's confession.

"What do we do now?" Lia asked.

"Every team requires a leader, a captain. I nominate E-Z," Alfred said.

"I second the nomination," Lia said.

Lia and Alfred raised their glasses to E-Z. Uncle Sam and Lia's mom Samantha joined in on the toast. Although they had no idea why they were all toasting to.

E-Z thanked them all. But inside he was wondering how it was all going to work. How, was he going to lead a little girl and a trumpeter swan? How was he going to keep them safe and out of harm's way?

Uncle Sam and Samantha offered to clean up, while the trio went back into the living room.

"It'll be a good opportunity for them to get to know each other a bit better," Alfred said.

"Yes, mother has never been this nervous before. With her job, she meets lots of people and she talks to them, even total strangers, like she's always known them. It's one of the secrets to her success, I think. With Sam though, she's as quiet as a mouse and jittery."

"Maybe it's jetlag," E-Z suggested.

Alfred laughed. "No, they are attracted to each other. You're both too young to notice, but there was a vibe in the air."

"Really, my mom has a crush on Sam?"

"Uncle Sam was awkward too– but he doesn't meet many girls these days since he works from home and spends most of his time helping me. I vote, we change the subject."

"Me too," Lia said.

"You two are no fun."

"I think it might be time for us to summon Eriel," E-Z said. "He must be the one who brought us all together. We need to be let in on the plan. To know what is going to be expected of us and when."

"Who is Eriel?" Lia asked. "I remember you asked me before if I knew him."

"He's an Archangel and he's been mentoring my trials. Well, the last few anyway."

"My angel, the one who has given me the gift of hand-sight, is named Haniel. She is an archangel too. She is the caregiver of the earth."

This surprised E-Z. If they were all working for their own angels, then why were they brought together? Was one angel more powerful than the other? Who was the boss angel? Who answered to whom?

"I'd sure like to know what's going on," Alfred said.

"All I know," Lia said, "is after the accident I was asked if I would be one of the three. And now, voila, here we are."

Uncle Sam and Samantha came into the room. They chatted for a while more together until Samantha who was tired from the flight went to her room. Uncle Sam also went to his room.

"Let's go in my room and talk," E-Z said.

Lia and Alfred followed. After a few hours of discussion, the trio realized they had lots of questions but few answers. Lia went to her room which she shared with her mother. Alfred slept on the edge of E-Z's bed. E-Z snored away. Tomorrow was another day – they'd figure it all out then.

CHAPTER THIRTEEN

THE NEXT MORNING LIA carried bowls of cereal out into the back garden. The sun was rising in the sky, it was a cloudless day and approaching 10 a.m. Alfred munched on the grass near the pathway.

Lia handed E-Z his bowl, then sat down under the umbrella on the patio and took a spoonful of Cornflakes.

"North American cornflakes taste different to the ones we have in the Netherlands."

"What's the difference?" E-Z asked.

"Everything here tastes sweeter."

"I've heard that they use different recipes in different countries. Do you want something else?" She declined with a shake of the head. "I couldn't sleep last night," E-Z said, taking another spoonful of Captain Crunch.

"Sorry, was I snoring too much?" Alfred inquired as he pushed his face in the dewy grass.

"No, you were fine. I had a lot on my mind. I mean, we're all here. The three – and I haven't had a trial in a while... Since Hadz and Reiki were demoted, I don't know what's going on. After that last battle with Eriel – which I won by the way – I haven't heard anything from Eriel. It's making me nervous. Wondering what he's dreaming up to make my life miserable."

Alfred waddled further away in the garden, as a unicorn landed on the grass.

"At your service," Little Dorrit said.

The unicorn nuzzled up to Lia, while she stood and kissed it on the forehead.

Above them a blue streak of skywriting began. It spelled out the words:

FOLLOW ME.

E-Z's chair rose, "Come on!" he cried.

Little Dorrit bowed down, allowing Lia to mount her.

Alfred flapped his wings and joined the others.

"Any idea where we're headed?" Alfred asked.

"All I know is we have to hurry! The vibrations are increasing so we must be close."

"Look up ahead," Lia cried. "Think we're needed at the amusement park."

Immediately, it was obvious to E-Z how they were needed. The roller coaster had been derailed. The cars were dangling half on and half off the tracks. And passengers of all ages were screaming. One kid was hanging so precariously with his legs over the side of the cart it was clear he'd fall first.

"We'll grab the kid," Lia said, taking off. She and Little Dorrit went straight for the boy. He let go, dropped, and landed safely in front of Lia on the unicorn.

"Thank you," the boy said. "Is this really a unicorn, or am I dreaming?"

"It really is," Lia said. "Her name is Little Dorrit."

"My mom has a book with that name. I think it's by Charles Dickens."

"That's right," Lia said.

"Are there unicorns in Little Dorrit? If yes, I'll have to read it!"

"I can't say for sure," Lia said. "But if you find out, let me know."

E-Z grabbed the overhanging cars one by one. It took some doing to balance it, it was a bit like a slinky all tilted in one direction at first. But his experience with the airplane helped and inspired him as he lifted the cars back onto the tracks. He held them steady until all the passengers were safely inside.

Thanks to the help of Alfred, this process was smooth. Alfred, using his wings, beak and sheer size was able to leverage them to safety.

"Is everyone okay?" E-Z called to resounding applause from all the passengers.

The task completed successfully, Alfred flew up to where Lia and the others were. It was an excellent location for observing.

"Is it okay for us to take the boy down now?" Lia asked.

E-Z gave her a thumbs up.

Below, a crane was brought in for the purpose of being raised up for a rescue. It wasn't anywhere near ready yet. He watched as workers scrambled around in their yellow hardhats.

E-Z whistled to the guy who operated the roller-coaster to start it up.

The roller-coaster operator restarted the engine. At first the cars chugged forward a bit, then stopped. The passengers screamed; in fear it would derail again. Some held their necks, which had been jarred in the original event.

E-Z positioned his wheelchair at the front of the cars to observe their position didn't alter. He noticed the wind was picking up, as passengers' hair was swept around in the cars. One elderly man lost his LA Dodgers baseball cap. Everyone watched as it plummeted to the ground.

"Try'er again," E-Z shouted, hoping for the best but thinking up a Plan B just in case.

The operator revved the engine. Once again, the roller-coaster moved forwards. This time a bit further, but again rolled to a full stop.

E-Z called out orders to Little Dorrit, "Please put Lia on the ground. Then grab some chain link with a hooks on both ends, and bring them up to me."

The unicorn nodded, descending to "oohs" and "ahhs" from the crowd which had gathered below. One guy tried to grab her and catch a ride, she pushed him away with her nose and the police moved in to cordon the area off.

"Here!" a construction worker said. He'd heard what E-Z requested. He placed part of the chain into Little Dorrit's mouth and circled the rest around her neck.

"It's not too heavy?" he asked, as Little Dorrit took off without any problem and winged her way up to where Alfred was now waiting at E-Z's side.

Alfred using his beak, put the hook into the front of the roller-coaster car. He secured it into place and attached it to E-Z's wheelchair.

"Please remain seated," E-Z called. "I'm going to get you down, slowly but surely. Try not to shift around too much, I'd like the weight to be consistently placed. On three, let's roll," he said. "One, two, three." He pulled, giving it everything he had, and the car rolled along with him. Going down was easy, coming up, he had to ensure the cart didn't pick up too much speed and get dislodged again. Little Dorrit and Alfred flew alongside the car, ready to act if anything went wrong.

Lia was so scared, nervous, and excited.

"You can do it, E-Z!" she shouted, forgetting she could speak the words in her head, and he'd hear them.

"Thanks," he said, keeping the pace slow and steady. Although E-Z was tired, he had to complete the task at hand. As the car rounded the corner and came to a full stop it went back into the tunnel. Back where its journey had first begun.

"Thank you!" the operator called.

Firefighters, paramedics, and nurses readied themselves for the onslaught of passengers. Disembarking at the same time.

"E-Z! E-Z! E-Z!" the crowd chanted, with phones raised filming the entire incident.

"Do you think we have time to grab some candy floss?" Lia asked.

"And Caramel Corn?" Alfred said. "I'm not sure if I'll like it, but I'm willing to give it a try!"

"Sure," E-Z said, "I'll get both for you no worries! Might even get myself a Candy Apple."

As he went to make the purchases, he noticed reporters had arrived. They were gathered around someone who was very tall with jet black hair. The man was holding a top hat in front of him and resembled Abraham Lincoln. Upon closer inspection he realized it was Eriel in disguise. He moved closer to listen in.

"Yes, I'm the one who brought together this dynamic trio. The leader is E-Z Dickens and he's thirteen years old and a superstar. Besides being the most experienced member of *The Three*, he's the leader. As you must have noticed, he can manage almost anything. He's a great kid!"

E-Z could feel his cheeks heating up.

"What about the girl and the unicorn?" a reporter called out.

"Her name is Lia, and this was her first venture in the superhero world. Her unicorn is Little Dorrit, and the two are an amazing team. She rescued that lad," he grabbed the boy. He put him front and centre for the cameras.

When every eye was on him, he finished his sentence. "With ease. Lia and Little Dorrit are wonderful additions to the team, and they'll be an immense help to E-Z in all his future endeavors."

"What was it like?" a reporter asked the boy.

"Lia was really nice," the young boy said.

The dark figured pushed the boy away. He dusted himself off.

"The trumpeter swan is named Alfred. This was his first opportunity to assist E-Z. He bravely, put himself at risk. Alfred is another excellent member of this superhero team of *The Three*. You'll be seeing a lot of them in the future." He hesitated, "Oh, and my name is Eriel, in case you want to quote me in your article."

Now E-Z wished he hadn't agreed to collect carnival treats. He cowered, off to the side, hoping not to get noticed.

"There he is!" someone shouted.

Others who were in line behind him, pushed him toward the front of the line.

"It's on the house," the seller said, handing him one of everything.

"Thank you," he said, as he lifted off.

"It's him! The boy in the wheelchair! Our hero!" someone shouted from below him.

"There he is, get his picture."

"Come on back for a selfie, please!"

E-Z glanced toward where Eriel had been, but now that he was spotted, no one was interested in him. Next thing he knew Eriel was gone.

"Let's get out of here!" E-Z exclaimed, wondering where exactly they should go. If they went to his house, the reporters and fans would more than likely follow. In a way, he missed the days when Hadz and

Reiki wiped the minds of everyone involved – it certainly uncomplicated things.

On the way back, E-Z couldn't help wondering what Eriel was up to. After all no one was supposed to know about his trials. It was very strange – but he was too exhausted to talk about it with his friends. Instead, he wondered why it was no longer important to keep his trials hidden – and how it was going to change things. It was good that his wings weren't burning anymore, and his chair didn't seem interested in drinking blood.

"Well, that was pretty easy," Alfred said.

Lia laughed, "And it was kind of fun, seeing you in action E-Z."

"Hey, what about me, I helped, too!"

"You sure did," E-Z said. "And Little Dorrit, thank you! Couldn't have done it without you!"

Little Dorrit laughed. "Glad to be of assistance."

"You were amazing!" Lia said, stroking her neck.

But something was troubling them. It was obvious, that E-Z could have done it all himself. He didn't need help.

Alfred especially felt like, being a trumpeter swan, he did all he could. But he wasn't much help in this kind of rescue. Not like someone who had hands could help. He had put in his best effort, but was it enough? Was he the best choice to be a member of *The Three*?

Lia was thinking that Little Dorrit could have landed under the boy and saved him without her being on its back. The unicorn was smart and could have followed E-Z's lead, and instructions. She felt like she'd come all this way, and for what? It didn't make any sense really.

They returned home again. Although they'd accomplished something wonderful together, their spirits were low.

Little Dorrit left and went off to wherever she lived when she wasn't needed.

E-Z immediately went to his office where he did a little work on his book. He'd been wanting to update the list of trials to see where he was. He decided to type them all in again from the beginning:

1/ rescued the little girl

2/ saved the plane from crashing

3/ stopped the shooter on the roof

4/ stopped the girl in the store

5/ stopped the shooter outside his house

6/ dueled with Eriel

7. got out of that bullet

8/ rescued Lia

9/ put a roller coaster back on track.

He wasn't sure if saving Uncle Sam was a trial or not. Hadz and Reiki had wiped his mind. E-Z's gut feeling was that saving Uncle Sam hadn't been a trial.

He sat back in his chair. Thinking about his impending deadline. He had to complete three more trials in a limited period. In one way, he wanted to get them done, over with. In another way, being finished with his commitment scared him.

Meanwhile, Alfred decided to go for a swim at the lake.

While, Lia, and her mother went for a walk.

"S O, WHAT WAS IT like?" Samantha asked.

"It was extremely exciting and scary at the same time. E-Z is remarkable. Fearless," Lia explained.

"And what was your contribution?"

They turned the corner and sat together on a park bench. Children played, running up and down and shouting. Both mother and daughter remembered how Lia used to play like this, carefree, when she was seven years old. Now that she was ten, her interest in playing had declined greatly.

"Do you, miss it?" Samantha asked.

Lia smiled. "You always know what I'm thinking. I don't really, but someday soon, I'd like to try dancing again. To see how and if I could adjust."

They sat together watching, without saying anything.

"As to my contribution, a little boy was hanging off the car and without Little Dorrit's help, might have fallen."

"Might have?"

"Yes, I think E-Z would have rescued him, then managed the rest, if we hadn't been there. He is used to doing the trials on his own."

"You don't think you or Alfred were needed?"

"Us being there for moral support was helpful, I don't know. The archangels have gone to a lot of trouble to get us together. To fly us all the way from the Netherlands, our home. When, based upon this trial, I don't think we are necessary."

Samantha took her daughter's hand into hers and they rose from the bench and turned back toward home.

"I think having a team, backup, is a good thing and I'm sure E-Z knows and appreciates it. He doesn't seem like the kind of kid to be a loner. He played baseball, still does from what Sam tells me. He knows teams work well together, building upon each player's strengths. As for you, I wouldn't worry that you weren't the most crucial factor in this trial. And never underestimate your worth."

"Thanks, Mom," Lia said, as they rounded the corner onto their street. "Now, let's talk about Sam. You really like him, don't you?"

Samantha smiled but did not answer.

AT THE SAME TIME, Sam was checking in on E-Z. "Is everything okay?" he asked, poking his head into his nephew's office.

"I'm not sure. Can we talk?"

"Sure thing, kiddo."

"Close the door, please."

"What's up? Didn't the first team trial go well?"

"First, I want to ask you, what's going on with you and Lia's Mom?"

Sam shuffled his feet and cleaned his glasses. "Let's not make this about me and Samantha. That's between us."

"Oh, so, there is an US, then?" he smirked.

"Change subject," Sam said.

"Okay then, whatever you say. As for the trial it went well, and don't think badly of me. I'm not saying this because I'm big-headed, but I could have completed it without the others."

"Tell me exactly what happened. What was your task? And I have to say, this surprises me, since you have always been a team player."

"I know. That's what's bothering me too. It was at the amusement park. A roller-coaster went off the track. The front of it was hanging off the edge and passengers were spilling over. Only one was in real danger – a kid who Lia caught with the help of Little Dorrit the unicorn."

"Sounds like that rescue was helpful."

"It was, cause the kid was of time, but I was there and could have rescued him. Then put the cart back on track and helped the others inside. It was like time stood still for me – so, I easily could have resolved this situation without anyone's help."

"It sounds like Alfred, wasn't much use to you. Are you inferring, you could do without him?"

E-Z ran his fingers through the dark middle of his hair. The bristly feeling somehow made him de-stress.

"Alfred helped. But I was looking for ways for him to help. He tries so hard. We so want to help, but honestly, he's smart enough to know I made work for him. So, he could help, and I don't feel good about it."

"That's what team players do. They look out for each other. Help each other."

"I know, but when there are lives at stake, it's up to me to make sure no one dies. If I'm finding tasks for the others to make them feel needed it's a handicap not help." He sighed deeply, clicking his fingers across his keyboard. Ashamed, he avoided eye contact with his uncle.

After a few minutes of silence, E-Z went back to working on his book to let his uncle mull things over. He went through the details of the day's events.

As he debriefed. Breaking things down. Taking the trial apart and putting it back together again he had a revelation. This was something he'd never done before. He could discuss the matter, with his team. They could tell him how he did, make suggestions so he could improve. Yes, there were many advantages to being one of the three. He felt relaxed and happier in this knowledge.

"I think you should give this team situation more time before you decide anything. It must be beneficial for you to know they each have their own special powers, to assist you. In this situation, your skills were at the forefront. That doesn't mean it will always be like this. Things could change for the next task. Everything happens for a reason."

"You're thinking along the same lines as I am now. Everything is always better if you don't have to face it alone. You taught me that."

"Anyone else in this house starving?" Alfred called as he waddled his way along the corridor.

E-Z pushed his chair back and answered, "Me!"

Sam said, "You what?"

"Oh, Alfred asked if anyone is hungry."

"Me too!" Sam called.

"I am," Lia said. "What's for dinner?"

Samantha suggested they order pizza. Everyone cheered, except for Alfred. He wasn't a fan of stringy cheese.

They spent the evening together, filling their faces and binge watching a series about zombies.

"It's not too scary for you, is it Lia?" E-Z asked,

"It's too scary for me!" Samantha replied. Sam put his arm around her, while Lia giggled and held her mother's hand.

CHAPTER FOURTEEN

Early next morning Alfred awoke with a scream. If you've never heard a swan scream, then you are lucky. It was so loud; it woke up everyone.

E-Z tried to calm Alfred down. The swan only flapped his wings more and made a terrible sound. It was like he was being tortured. Either that or the world was ending!

Uncle Sam arrived to check what was happening.

"It's Alfred, but don't worry. I've got this," E-Z said.

Soon Lia and Samantha came to investigate. Lia convinced Samantha to go back to sleep.

Lia remained, to help E-Z comfort Alfred. Who immediately went to the window, opened it with his beak and flew out into the night.

Above them, E-Z and Lia listened to Alfred's webbed feet slapped on the roof.

"What are you two waiting for!" he shouted. "We need to go – NOW!"

Lia climbed out the window and stood shivering on the ledge. She waited until E-Z was able to get into his wheelchair and to maneuver it into a hovering position.

"Wait, I think the unicorn is finally on the way," Alfred said. "That's why I am up here. To see if she was coming."

Little Dorrit landed, put her nose under Lia and tossed her onto her back.

Off they flew with Alfred leading the way.

"Slow down!" E-Z shouted. Alfred ignored him. He continued, picking up altitude and speed. E-Z's chair wings began flapping as did his angel wings. He had to work fast to keep Alfred in sight.

Lia shivered. "I wish I had a sweater with me."

"Snuggle up to my neck," Little Dorrit said. "I'll keep you warm."

E-Z picked up the pace, closing in, then realized Alfred was slowing down. Or so he thought. Instead, he saw a sight which would never be erased from his mind. Alfred was frozen in mid-air, with his wings and feet extended. Like he was modelling as an X.

Then his entire body started trembling, which grew to a shake. It looked like he was being electrocuted. And his face, the expression of unbearable pain on it, brought a tear to his friends' eyes.

"What's happening to him?" Lia asked. "I can't watch it anymore. I just can't," she sobbed.

"It's like he's being shocked. Who would do such a thing?" As he said it, he knew. Only Eriel could be this cruel. Eriel was summoning them. Using this electrocution technique to make them follow their friend Alfred. Only, what if he didn't survive the shocks? As he said this, a handful of Alfred's feathers disconnected from his body and floated in the air. He stopped shaking and started flying. Over his shoulder he said, "Come on, keep up before it hits me again."

"Are you okay?" Lia asked.

"That was the third one, and each time it gets worse. We need to get where they want us to be and fast. I don't know if I can live through another one – not worse than the last one. It was a doozy."

They flew on, chatting as they went.

"I'm sorry for waking everyone up," Alfred said now that the shocks had ceased.

"It wasn't your fault." E-Z said. "I'm pretty sure I know whose fault it is – and when we see him, I'm going to give him the what for."

"What do you mean?" Lia asked, snuggling into Little Dorrit's neck. It was so dark and cold; she couldn't stop shivering.

Alfred said, "We have been summoned by sending electric shocks throughout my body. It was like my feathers were on fire from the inside out. So rude. So very rude and for a minute, I thought I was back in the betwixt and the between again."

His entire swan body trembled thinking about it. "I'll give whoever did it what they deserve when I see them too!"

Alfred continued flying abreast of the others. "Previously Ariel whispered in my ear to wake me up. Then we'd talk out a plan together. She even did this when I was in the betwixt and the between. She has always been gentle and kind to me. This summons was different."

"Sounds like Eriel's doing," E-Z admitted. "He's not very tactful and he can be a bit melodramatic and quite insensitive. Not to mention he has a sick sense of humour."

"A bit melodramatic, does not even scratch the surface," Alfred said.

"You'll have to tell us more about this betwixt and between sometime. The name sounds cute, but I have a feeling it's an oxymoron," E-Z said.

"I don't like to talk about it," Alfred replied.

"I'm really looking forward to meeting this Eriel person. NOT." Lia confessed. "It's like looking forward to meeting Voldemort. His reputation precedes him."

"Ah, a Harry Potter fan, then?" Alfred said.

"Definitely," Lia admitted.

The stars in the sky above sent out imaginary heat. Still, they shivered unprepared in the night air.

"Are we nearly there?" E-Z asked.

"I don't know for sure," Alfred said. "The shock didn't say where we were summoned to, and I can't pick up on any vibrations in the air. The only thing that will indicate we're not doing what is expected of us, is another shock. Unfortunately."

"We don't want that to happen. Let's pick up the pace."

"It seems we are getting closer though." Alfred stopped mid-air; wings fully extended. "Oh no!" he whispered, waiting for the new shock to hit. He waited and waited but nothing happened. "Guess we're nearly…"

The swan's body did not only shake and tremble this time. Alfred's body rolled over and over again. Like he was performing somersaults in the sky.

Lose feathers flew around him, dancing in the wind as the swan went into freefall.

E-Z flew under the trumpeter swan and caught him. "Alfred? Alfred?" The poor swan had fainted. "Eriel! You! You big hairy vulture!" E-Z shouted, raising his fist toward the sky. "You don't have to kill Alfred. Tell us where you are, and we will be there, but only if you agree to knock it off with the electrical charges. It's barbaric. He's a swan for pity's sake. Give him a break."

"What he said," Lia replied, with her open palms facing skyward.

For a second, they hovered, still in place.

Then a shock hit the wheelchair. Then it hit Dorrit the unicorn. And everyone went into freefall.

Eriel's laughter filled the air around them. The world was his Sensurround, and he mocked *The Three* like no one else could. Or would.

CHAPTER FIFTEEN

THEY CONTINUED PLUMMETING FOR quite some time. None of them had any control of their special powers or attributes.

They were half expecting their bodies would be splattered on the pavement below. The pavement was rising to greet them.

Suddenly, the descent ended. It was like they were all attached to some invisible puppeteer.

After a few seconds, movement restarted But this time it was gentle.

Guiding them, until they could safely be dropped at the feet of Eriel, Ariel and Haniel the archangels.

"Have a nice trip?" Eriel asked. He bellowed with laughter. His companions looked on without laughing or speaking.

Alfred, now awake flew and landed, followed by Little Dorrit the Unicorn carrying Lia.

The unicorn bowed to the other guests, then retreated to the far side of the room.

Eriel was the tallest of the other three was standing with his hands on his hips, making certain that there was no question as to who was in charge.

Ariel in contrast was fairy-like.

Haniel was statuesque, radiating beauty.

Eriel stepped forward, lifted off the ground so he was above them. He bellowed, "It took you long enough to get here! In the future when I command your presence you will be here lickety-split!"

Haniel flew closer to Alfred. She touched him on the forehead. She then turned to E-Z and did the same. She smiled. "Happy to meet you both." She turned to Lia. Lia opened her palm and the two exchanged open palm finger touches. Lia threw herself into Haniel's arms. Haniel wrapped her wings around her, taking in the new ten-year-old girls' appearance.

Ariel fluttered close to E-Z. She winked at him and smiled at Lia. She flew to Alfred and relieved him of his pain.

"Enough fussing!" Eriel commanded with his voice thundering so loud that E-Z feared he would raise the roof.

"Wait a minute," Alfred said, walking with the sound of his webbed feet flapping on the concrete floor. "I was nearly electrocuted, and I'd like an apology."

Eriel opened his wings wide, wider, as wide as they could go. He hovered above Alfred who shivered but held his ground. Their eyes locked.

E-Z felt that Alfred the trumpeter swan was either very brave or very foolish. Either way, he needed help.

E-Z rolled forward, positioned his chair between them. "What's done is done." He addressed Alfred, "Stand down." Alfred did. Then to Eriel, "I know you are a bully and what you did to our friend was unforgiveable and cruel. It's the middle of the night so get to the point – tell us why are we here? What's the big emergency?"

Eriel landed and his wings folded in behind his body. He bellowed, "My attempts to reach you personally my protégé went unanswered. No matter what I did, your snoring kept you from waking. I sent Haniel for

Lia, but she was unable to awaken her without disturbing her mother who was sleeping next to her. Therefore, we summoned Alfred who also did not respond for quite some time. His mentor tried to approach him, in her usual fashion – but her whispers weren't powerful enough to wake him up."

"I was worried about you," Ariel said.

"I'm sorry," Alfred said. "E-Z's bed is wonderfully comfortable, and he does snore quite loudly. It had been a long while since I slept in an actual bed again."

"SILENCE!" Eriel screeched.

Alfred stepped back, whereas E-Z moved his chair that much closer to creature.

Eriel lowered his voice. "Haniel thought you were dead, swan. And therefore I, used this opportunity to assess our newest technology."

"It hadn't been performed on humans before," Haniel admitted.

"We thought it would be best to try on someone who wasn't human – Alfred you fit the bill and it worked a charm. True, all of you were tardy in your arrival, but you got here. As they say, better late than never."

"You used me as a guinea pig?" Alfred said, swinging his neck back and forth with his beak wide open and advancing across the floor.

E-Z once again positioned his wheelchair between them. "Stand down," he said to Alfred.

Eriel, Haniel and Ariel formed a semi-circle around the trio.

"You're right E-Z. What's done is done. Better they tried it on me, than on the two of you. Now get on with it," Alfred demanded.

"Yes, Eriel," E-Z said, "again I ask, why are we here?"

"First of all," the archangel bellowed, "the plan was for the three of you to form a trio of sorts."

"We already figured that out for ourselves," Lia said. She was holding her palms open so she could take in the full view of the three archangels at the same time. She also looked around the room from time to time to take in their surroundings. It looked familiar, with metal walls like the one she'd first met E-Z in. Only much more spacious.

E-Z looked around and looked at Lia. He was thinking the same thing. The more he looked at the walls, the more they seemed to close in on him. He felt cold, and claustrophobic even though the space was huge. He wished his wheelchair had a button like in some cars where the seat could be heated.

"Silence!" Eriel shouted. Since all were silent, it seemed out of place. Of course, they hadn't taken into consideration that he could also read their thoughts.

Alfred laughed.

Eriel closed the gap between them, and Alfred backed up. Eriel closed the gap again. And so, on and so on until Alfred was backed up against the wall. Alfred took flight. Eriel picked him up with his talon-like feet. Held him above the others.

"Eriel, please," Ariel said. "Alfred is a good soul."

Eriel put him down, then raised his fists. Bolts of lightning flew out of them and ricocheted off the metal ceiling of the container. All but Eriel played dodgem with the flying electrical charges. Eriel watched. Laughed. Until he was tired of the entertainment.

The Three's confidence had been put to the test.

Eriel caught the remaning lightning bolts. He made a big show of it, as he placed them into his pockets.

"Now then," he said with a sly grin. "A new trial is coming your way. Today. One of you will die."

E-Z bolted up in his chair. Alfred screamed an involuntary "Hoo-hoo!" and Lia screamed a little girl scream.

Eriel continued, ignoring their reactions. "You are here to choose. Which one of you will die today? After you choose, I will explain the consequences which you will face due to said death." Eriel flew a few feet away and the other two angels were beside him, one on each side.

First, Ariel described Alfred's death:

"I cannot tell you about any details for this trial. All I can tell you, is that Alfred, should you die today, you will not fulfill your contractual agreement. Therefore, you will not see your family again, not now or ever. Your death, however, would be beautiful. For as in life, the death of a swan is always beautiful. Majestic. For when a swan dies, it does become an angel. Your transformation would be a new beginning for you. Your purpose would be for the betterment of humans and animals alike. You would be given a new name and a new purpose. You would be truly valued in every way. And your soul would return to its everlasting resting spot."

Tears streamed down Alfred's trumpeter swan cheeks. Ariel comforted him by wrapping her wings around his wings.

Second, Haniel told of Lia's death:

"Child, soon to become a woman, like Ariel, I cannot tell you any information about the task at hand. All I can say to you dear Cecelia, also known as Lia, is that should you died today, then you will no longer be. In any form. Your death will be just that, a death. Final. It will be like it would have been when the lightbulb exploded, you would have died. Your poor life would have ended then. And yet you are here now, and you have much to offer the world. You have not even scratched upon the surface of the powers available to you. However, should you die today those powers would remain unspent. You would go into the ground, dust to dust. A mere memory to those who have known and loved you. But your soul also, would return to its everlasting resting place."

Lia closed her hands to contain the tears falling from them. They were also falling from the eyes. Her old eyes. Her body shuddered when she sobbed. She was too overwrought with emotion to speak.

Little Dorrit moved in and nudged the little girl on the shoulder. Haniel also tried to comfort her by kissing her on the forehead.

And then Eriel began telling E-Z's story:

"E-Z, you have achieved many things since your parents died. Trials have been given to you. Sometimes, often insurmountable tasks for a human. Yet you have been successful in overcoming them. You have saved lives. You have not disappointed me. However, we do feel." She hesitated glancing side to side. "I especially feel that you have thwarted your powers. Sometimes even denied them. You have taken the time we have given you to make the world a better place and squandered it."

E-Z opened his mouth to speak.

"Silence!" Eriel screamed. "Don't try to justify yourself. We've been watching you playing baseball and wasting time with friends like you had all the time in the world to complete your tasks. Well, time is up. If you die today, your trials would be incomplete."

E-Z had a good idea what was coming next, but he had to wait for Eriel to say it. To speak the words for it to be true.

As he surmised, Eriel wasn't finished yet. "Leaving us with incomplete trials for which your life was saved. Now that would be unforgiveable. If you died today, you would lose your wings. That's for starters. Those trials that you hadn't been given yet - would never be. For you were the only one who could complete the tasks. Our only hope.

"Therefore, those who you would have saved would not be saved by anyone, at any time. They will die because of you. Everyone you ever saved during your trials would die.

"It would be as if you never existed. Their deaths would be final. Complete. Zero opportunity for an afterlife for any of them. Even sending them to the betwixt and the between would not be an option. Your death then E-Z would wreak havoc and bring chaos to the world. Like on the day you and I dueled. Remember what the world was like on that day? That is how the earth would be – on every single day." Eriel turned his back. They watched him extend his wings, like he was preparing to leave.

All were silent. Contemplating their fates.

After some time, Eriel broke the silence. "Ariel, Haniel and I will leave you for now. You can talk amongst yourselves and decide. But be quick about it. We don't have all day."

The trio of archangels disappeared through the ceiling.

CHAPTER SIXTEEN

After the archangels left, *The Three* were too stunned to say anything. Until E-Z broke the silence.

"It makes no sense to me, for them to bring us all here together. For them to torture Alfred. Get us here. Then tell us one of us must die. And we have to choose which one. It's barbaric – even for Eriel."

Lia paced with her fists clenched. She was too angry to speak, and she didn't care if she bumped into anything. In fact, when she did, she kicked it

.

Alfred chimed in. "I think if anyone has to die, it should be me. My powers are extremely limited. I'd more than likely get turned into swan soup given the complexities of the trials. Like the last trial. I know you were helping me E-Z. It was kind of you, but I knew I was a liability."

E-Z tried to interrupt but Alfred just barreled on. "Not to mention, I might get in the way. Put one of you at risk. I've lived a sad and lonely life since my family were taken from me. Someday the loneliness is overwhelming. Being a member of *The Three* has helped but..."Even as a swan, I could think of them. Remember them, love them. Just knowing that they died together and are somewhere together gives me peace. Even if I'm not with them, But I will be today, if I am the one to die. I'm willing to take that risk. Besides, when I go no one on earth will miss m e."

"We will miss you!" Lia said.

"Of course, we'll miss you!" E-Z agreed, as he crossed the floor, noticing a table which before had blended into the wall. He moved closer to it, on which he discovered a stack of papers which he flipped through.

"I appreciate the sentiment," Alfred said. "Hey, what are you doing, E-Z? Where did that table come from?"

Lia held both hands out in front of her so she could see both E-Z and Alfred simultaneously.

E-Z continued flipping pages. Soon they were flying all around the room. Spinning in the air like they had been caught in the eye of a tornado.

The Three grouped together and watched the flurry of paper. Then at all once they dropped onto the pavement.

Lia grabbed one of them and read it while E-Z and Alfred looked on.

"What is this?" she exclaimed. "It says our names. It tells the stories. Our stories. Of our deaths."

"It says we are already dead!" E-Z said reading one of the papers he'd snafued.

"Oh," Lia said, with a tear running down her cheek. "It also says my mother is dead as is your Uncle Sam."

E-Z shook his head. "It can't be true. It's not true. They are playing us." He looked around. Something in the room had changed. The walls. They were now red. "Have we gone into another dimension or something? Look at the walls? Are we somewhere else, where the future is already the past?"

Alfred picked up another one of the fallen pages. It told of the death of his wife, his children and of his own death. And yet, when he looked at himself, felt himself, he was alive, with feathers: a trumpeter swan. "I want out," he said.

Lia smiled. "Do you mean, out of this room, or out of this life? I want out too, I mean out of this creepy metal container, but I don't want to die. Seeing the world through the palms of my hands is weird and cool at the same time. Being able to read thoughts, that's cool too. When I stopped time though, that was awesome. Imagine being able to summon that power, like if someone was in danger, or if there was a disaster. Imagine how many lives could be saved? And now I'm ten and who knows what other powers there are in store for me."

"Godlike," E-Z said. "I know how you felt Lia. That's how I felt too, when I saved that first little girl, when I saved the others and when I saved you."

The three reformed a circle and joined hands as they recited the words, "We have the power. No one dies today. No matter what they say." They turned around and around, chanting their new mantra. Until they were ready to summon the archangels back again.

CHAPTER SEVENTEEN

ERIEL ARRIVED FIRST, WITH his eyebrows raised and his lip twisted into a scorn. Next Ariel and Haniel arrived. The two remained behind him in the shadow of his enormous wings. Eriel crossed his arms, while the two other archangels moved up. They hovered on opposite sides of his shoulders.

"We have decided," E-Z said. "No one will die today."

Eriel's laughter thundered around the metal enclosure. He rose into the air, then crossed his arms over his chest. Ariel and Haniel remained silent, while Eriel's laughter increased in pitch, high enough to hurt Alfred's ears.

Alfred fainted but recovered quickly. Lia and E-Z helped him up. They held him up until Little Dorrit flew over. Moments later Alfred was sitting high above them on the unicorn. He was face to face with Eriel.

"Thanks, mate," Alfred said.

"Glad to be of assistance," Little Dorrit said.

"Enough!" Eriel shouted, moving higher above them. Intimidating them with his size, his morbidity, his thundering voice. "You think you can change what will be? I have told you what must happen, and you have no choice but to obey me. It wasn't a survey. Nor a democracy. It was a certitude. For it is written..."

Then he noticed that the floor was covered with papers. He flew down and picked one up. Then rose up, so he was face to face with Alfred. In his hand he was holding Alfred's story.

"I see you have read the future. Now you know the truth, that you are living in a parallel universe. What happens here, ripples throughout the other universes. In places where both the future and the past exist."

Lia dropped her right hand and held up her left. Her arms were not strong, for they were still getting used her having to hold them up.

Eriel flew across the room to a red sofa which he sat upon. The other angels joined him, one on each of the arms. Eriel sat comfortably with his wings neither fully in nor out.

After he made himself comfortable, he continued. "In one of the worlds, all three of you are already dead. You read the truth. In this world, there is still hope. Hope exists, because of us, that is me, Ariel, Haniel and Ophaniel. We have chosen you three humans, to collaborate with us. We have given you goals, and we have assisted you where and when we can. While we are with you, we alone are allowing your existence to continue. We alone are giving your life purpose. Refuse to follow the path we've chosen for you, and you shall no longer exist here in this world either. You will be erased, like you never were and never would be."

E-Z clenched his fists and his chair lurched forwards. "In the document, the document about my other life, it stated that Uncle Sam was dead too. He wasn't in the accident with my parents. He's not a part of this bargain. Did you kill him Eriel, to keep me here?"

Without waiting for an answer Lia chimed in. "In my document, it says that my mother is dead. How can that be true? Please tell me it's not true!"

Alfred now feeling better, jumped off Little Dorrit's back. He waddled closer to the sofa and again came face to face with Eriel.

E-Z looked on proudly, at his friend Alfred the fearless trumpeter swan.

"And in the documents, my prayers are answered. I am dead already. I died with my family as it should have been. I'd rather have been left dead. To have died with them, instead of being reincarnated as a trumpeter swan. That's after Haniel rescued me from the betwixt and the between."

Eriel shooed Alfred away. "Ah, yes, the betwixt and the between. I'd forgotten you were sent there. Not so fond of it were you?"

Alfred moved his neck and grimaced with his beak. He bared his small, jagged teeth like he wanted to bite Eriel.

"Stand down," E-Z said as he rolled up to the sofa.

Alfred closed his beak. Lia moved in closer. Now *The Three* were standing together in front of Eriel. They waited for the archangel to say something, anything. For once speechless.

E-Z took the opportunity to get the situation in hand.

"In the papers, it stated that Uncle Sam had died in the accident with my mother, my father and me. He wasn't in the car with us, for this to have occurred, he would have had to have been planted in the vehicle with us. For what purpose? Explain to us you so called archangels. Why would you change history to suit your own purposes? Where is God in all this by the way? I want to speak to him."

"So, do I!" Lia exclaimed.

"Me too!" Alfred chimed in.

Eriel crossed his legs and spread his wings. He put his hand on his chin and answered, "God has nothing to do with us or you – not anymore." He yawned, like this task was boring him.

"What if I told you that your house was on fire as we speak? What if I told you that neither Uncle Sam, nor your mother Samantha, Lia would live to see another day?"

"You b-b-bastard!" E-Z exclaimed.

"Ditto!" Lia said.

"Come now," Eriel chided. "We are all friends here. Friends, aren't we? Your house could be on fire, anything could happen while we are here in this place, suspended in time. The longer you delay from choosing, the more chaos you create in the world." He stood and his wings extended, causing the trio to take a few steps back.

He continued, "E-Z you would risk your life for your Uncle Sam, correct?" He nodded. "Of course, you would. And Lia, you'd risk your life to save your mother's life, yes?" Lia nodded.

"And Alfred, my dear little trumpeter swan. My feathery deathery friend. Which of the two would you save. If you could save only one of them?" Eriel smiled, proud of the rhymes he'd made.

"I'd save them both," Alfred said. "I'd risk my life or die trying."

"You have a strange death wish my feathered friend."

Alfred barreled toward Eriel.

"Y-o-u a-r-e n-o-t m-y f-r-i-e-n-d! Stop playing games with us. You brought us together. Why? To taunt us. To make a little girl cry. You're nothing but a, but a big bully."

"Yes," Lia said. "Stop bullying us."

"What they said," E-Z added.

Eriel now furious, turned from black to red to black to red. He flew across the room and slammed his fists down on the table.

"You want the truth? You can't handle the truth!" He smirked. "A little sidebar, I love Jack Nicholson's performance in *A Few Good Men*."

It was one thing both Eriel and E-Z agreed upon. Nicholson's performance in that movie was flawless.

"Stop the melodramatics and tell us what you want from us."

"We already did," Eriel said. "I told you one of you must die today. I told you to choose which one. It is written, one of you must die. You must choose. Now."

Alfred stepped forward, with his swan neck extended. "Then it will be me."

Alfred kneeled, his body trembling. He lowered his head, like he expected the archangel to chop it off.

Instead, all three archangels applauded. They romped around the room. Screeching like they were hired clowns performing at a children's birthday party.

After a few minutes of complete madness, the archangels stopped.

"It is done," Eriel said.

And then they were gone.

CHAPTER EIGHTEEN

WITH E-Z IN HIS wheelchair, Lia on Little Dorrit, and Alfred the swan still *The Three* as they soared across the sky. They continued onwards for some miles, until below them they noticed a huge metal bridge.

A young man teeter-tottered on the ledge giving every indication that he was going to jump.

E-Z took his phone out and was set to call 911, while Alfred, without hesitation flew down to the man. He put his phone away and he and Lia followed.

Alfred hovered near the man, unable to speak and be understood by him all he could say was, "Hoo-hoo!"

"Get away from me!" the man shouted, waving poor Alfred who was only trying to help away.

The man inched his way closer to the edge, kicking off his shoes and watching them drop into the river below him. He watched, as the water overtook them, pulling the shoes under with its hungry mouth. Wanting to see more, he removed his t-shirt - which ironically said, "The End," on the front of it.

The young man looked on as his favourite shirt swayed and danced on its way down. As the water swallowed it up, the man began to sing:

"Here I go round the mulberry bush.

The mulberry bush, the mulberry bush.

Here I go round the mulberry bush,

All on a, on a sunny, morning."

Alfred heard him singing. He was familiar with the rhyme. He waited for the man to sing another verse. In fact, he wanted him to sing more. But he was afraid to disturb him. The man wouldn't understand, even if he tried to talk to him.

By this time, E-Z was waiting for a sign from Alfred. Finally, he got one – Alfred told him and Lia not to come any closer.

Alfred wished the young man could understand him. If he moved nearer, could he catch him? He moved closer, expanding his wings to the fullest.

The young man saw him. "Swan," he said. Then he jumped.

The trumpeter swan was bigger than the average swan. But not big enough to catch a full-grown man. He tried though, to break his fall. He put his life in jeopardy to save him. But no matter what he did, the man still dropped like a lead balloon. Into the hungry mouth of the river.

Alfred without a thought for himself, dove in after him. How he intended to carry the man out, no one knew. Some say it's the thought that counts. In this case, Alfred was pulled under by the sheer weight of the man.

By this time, E-Z was hovering above the water, looking for either the man or Alfred to surface so he could help them. Neither Lia, nor Little Dorrit knew how to swim. And E-Z couldn't go in for them with or without his chair.

Exasperated he flew toward the shore, looking for any sign of life. At last, he saw it, something bobbing on the other side. He rushed over, carried the man to where Lia waited, and once he was coughing, went to look for any signs of Alfred the swan.

Then he saw him. Half in and half out of the water. Bobbing along with the tide.

"Alfred!" he called, as he lifted the swan's head, noticing immediately that his neck was broken. Alfred the trumpeter swan, his friend was no more. Eriel's deed was done.

Lia, who had been watching E-Z's every move, saw Alfred's neck and screamed "Nooooooo!"

E-Z lifted the swan's lifeless body onto his wheelchair and held it. He too began to cry.

Behind them, the man who Alfred saved called out,

"I'm not dead! It's me, Alfred."

CHAPTER NINETEEN

E ARTH PAUSE.

Birds stopped mid-flight. As did planes. And other flying objects such as balloons and drones. Bullets stopped firing after they'd exited the chamber. Water ceased flowing over Niagara Falls. Bugs no longer buzzed. The air stood still.

Ophaniel appeared, alongside of Eriel, Ariel and Haniel. With her hands on her hips, and her chin thrust forward, it was more than obvious that she was annoyed.

Instead of speaking, she turned in the direction of E-Z.

He was frozen, his mouth wide open. His last spoken word had been, "NOOOOOOOOOOOOOOOOOO!"

Now she observed Lia. The girl had a tear frozen on her cheek. It had flowed from her old eye.

Now back to E-Z. He carried a body. The body of a dead swan.

Now, to Alfred, who was no longer a swan. He'd taken on the form of a man. A drowned man.

The very man who was to replace him in *The Three*.

"Now, what's wrong with this picture?" Ophaniel the ruler of the moon of the stars inquired.

No one dared to speak.

"Eriel, you're in charge here. First, you mess up the bonding test with E-Z and Sam by getting yourself, pardon the expression – batted out of the park.

"Now, through your stupidity, Alfred the swan has taken over a human body. The body of the person who I told you, should be a member of *The Three*.

"You know what we're up against. You understand what the future holds if we don't get things in order. You know!"

Eriel bowed at the feet of Ophaniel, then lifted off the ground before speaking. "I spoke the words, it is done."

"Yes, you spoke the words and then you failed to ensure the task was completed you imbecile!"

She hovered near the new Alfred. "I'm sorry, but this complicates things, even for us. Even with our powers, getting him out of this human body and back into his swan form won't be as easy. We might have to send him back to the betwixt and the between! And he doesn't deserve that. In fact,"

Ariel flew to Ophaniel's side and asked, "May I speak?"

"You may, if you have any insight into Alfred which may help us out of this mess."

"I know Alfred, better than anyone here. He did agree to be the one, to sacrifice himself. He'd do it again without a moment's hesitation – even if there wasn't anything in it for him. That is one huge sacrifice for any living creature to make, to give his life to save another. Also, it should be considering how much Alfred has been made to suffer, both in his human existence and as a swan. He's an exceptional soul and he should be given a second chance, and a third, and more!"

Eriel scoffed, "He should be gone, back to the betwixt and the between for all eternity. He's not worthy of..."

"I didn't give you permission to interrupt!" Ophaniel screamed. To keep him from interrupting in future she buttoned his lips shut.

"This is true, what you are saying, Ariel," Ophaniel said. "Alfred collaborates well with both Lia and E-Z. We ought to give him a second chance in this new body. He wasn't meant to be in the betwixt and the between. It was down to Hadz and Reiki. We'd have banished them to the mines straightaway after that. Instead, we gave them another chance with E-Z.

"Still, Eriel did send them to the mines. So, all's well that ends well. Perhaps, Alfred does deserve another chance. Let's see what happens, as humans say, play it by ear. If it works out fine. If not, this body can be recycled since the spirit has already left the building."

"Thank you," Ariel said, bowing low to Ophaniel. "Thank you so much. I'll keep an eye on the situation. I won't let Alfred let you down."

Ophaniel nodded, lifted off and said the words:

EARTH RESUME.

Time began ticking and the world went back to the way it was before.

Ophaniel disappeared first, the other three waited a few seconds before they followed.

CHAPTER TWENTY

"NO WAY!" E-Z EXCLAIMED, wheeling himself closer to the new Alfred. "Alfred, is it you? Can it, really be you?"

Lia didn't have to ask because she already knew. She ran to Alfred and threw her arms around him.

Alfred said, in his English accent, "Eriel must've done a switch-a-roo."

Alfred, who was only wearing a pair of jeans, shivered. "Although I'm freezing cold, it sure feels good to be back in a body again." He flexed his muscles and ran on the spot to warm himself up. Then he did a few cartwheels across the lawn while E-Z and Lia stood watching with their mouths hanging open.

"What a show-off!" Little Dorrit said.

Alfred who'd just noticed her, went over, and ran his hand along her fur. She felt so soft and warm, he nuzzled up into her.

"This is a rather strange turn of events," E-Z said, wheeling nearer. "I don't know quite what to make of it."

"I don't know either," Alfred said, "But can we discuss it while we're eating? I'm starving and a cheeseburger loaded with ketchup and onions with a giant side of fries would sure hit the spot."

"Wait a minute," E-Z said. "If you're this guy, this guy whose name we don't even know – then what if someone recognizes you?"

Alfred bent down and touched his toes. He felt the skin on his face. His hair. "We'll cross that bridge when we get to it." He smiled, lifted his head in the direction of the sky and said, "Thank you Eriel, wherever you are."

A plane over their heads skywrote the words:

Once more unto the breach, dear friends.

"That's a rather strange phrase for skywriting," Lia observed. "Either of you know what it means?"

E-Z shook his head, "I can google it." He pulled out his phone.

"No need," Alfred said. "It's from Shakespeare, attributed to King Henry. Literally it means, 'Let us try one more time.' I believe it was said during battle. So, I'm assuming this is a message from my Ariel, letting me know that I've been given another chance." Tears welled up in his e yes.

E-Z was suspicious of this change of events. He was happy Alfred was still with them, but he wondered what at what price. "I'm worried," E-Z admitted.

Lia said she was too.

"Ah, don't worry. If Ariel sends me this message, then she is on our side. Besides, the man whose body I'm in – he didn't want it anymore. I tried to save him, but he jumped anyway. Perhaps it's fate, for me to help you with your trials E-Z. Whatever it is, I'll take it. I'll give it my all. That's after I'm in a shirt and some shoes."

"I wonder what your powers are now Alfred. I mean, if you still have them, or if you have other powers. Or none. Since you're human again," Lia asked.

Alfred scratched his blond-haired head. "Uh, I don't know. The only thing needing a cure around here is my former swan body. I don't want to take a chance if I cure it, I'll end up back in it."

"Fair enough," Lia said. "But we can't leave your old swan body there, now, can we? We have to bury it."

As they looked upon the lifeless body, it disappeared into thin air.

"Well, that solves the problem," E-Z said.

"I feel like I ought to say some words, for the passing of my old body. Does anyone mind?"

Both E-Z and Lia bowed their heads.

Alfred recited an excerpt from the poem by Lord Alfred Tennyson entitled:

The Dying Swan:

The plain was grassy, wild, and bare,
Wide, wild, and open to the air,
Which had built up everywhere
An under-roof of doleful gray.
With an inner voice the river ran,
Adown it floated a dying swan,
And loudly did it lament.

Here Alfred Hoo-Hoo'd and Hoo-Hoo'd until tears filled all their eyes as the poem continued:

It was the middle of the day.
Ever the weary wind went on,
And took the reed-tops as it went.
They stood together in a moment of silence.

Then Lia said, "Now let's get you some fresh and dry clothes, then we'll all go to a burger joint. I'm hungry and thirsty too."

E-Z shook his head. "Some food would be good, but I'm still suspicious of Eriel. Something here isn't adding up."

"We'll figure it out – once we've eaten! Lead me to cheeseburger heaven."

They started moving along the promenade of the waterfront. They continued walking for some time. Before they realized they were lost.

"I am an excellent navigator," Little Dorrit the unicorn said, as she flew down to greet them. "Climb aboard Alfred and Lia. E-Z you may follow me."

Alfred reached into his jeans pocket and pulled out a wallet. Inside he found a few bills and the identification of the body in which he now resided. The young man's name was David, James Parker, aged twenty-four. He held up a driver's license.

"Nice photo," Lia said.

"Yes, I am rather handsome."

"Oh, brother," E-Z said, pushing onward.

Up, up into the air Little Dorrit's passengers flew. E-Z followed until he knew where he was. He decided to ask for a GPS to be added to his wheelchair. Pity they hadn't thought about it when they modded it.

The descent followed by a quick trip into a second-hand shop. Alfred now wore a new t-shirt, jeans, runners, and socks. Followed by a short line up before the ordering of food began.

Little Dorrit made herself scarce, while the trio tucked into their food. They were all very hungry.

Alfred made cooing noises, too many to describe in much detail. When they finished eating, they deposited the rubbish in their appropriate bins. And made their way home.

When they were almost there, Alfred called out to E-Z, "We need to talk!"

"Can't this wait until you land?" Little Dorrit asked. "After I'm finished here, I have places, to go, people to see."

"How rude," E-Z said. "Go ahead, Alfred or David or whatever your name is now."

"That's what I wanted to talk to you about," Alfred said. "How are you going to explain my transformation to Uncle Sam and Samantha? Uh, Uncle Sam, and Samantha, I'd like you to meet Alfred the trumpeter swan. His name is now David James Parker. Thanks to the body he entered and currently resides in. Since the young man who was the previous owner of the body committed suicide. On the Jones Street Bridge."

"Oh geez," E-Z said. "It's one hundred percent the truth as we know it, but we can't tell them the truth."

"My mother would faint if we said that. Why don't we tell them that Alfred the swan flew south? For sunnier weather. Or that he met a mate? Then we can introduce Alfred as D.J., which sounds much more friendly than David James."

"You're a genius," E-Z said "Although, since my friend is called PJ, things could get a bit confusing with a DJ and PJ. What do you think Alfred? Do you have a preference?"

"I don't like DJ. It sounds way too common. I'd prefer to be called Parker. Parker the Butler was one of my favourite characters on Thunderbirds."

"Parker it is then," E-Z finished saying as Lia let out a scream and Alfred fainted – their home was gone. Burned to the ground.

CHAPTER TWENTY-ONE

"Oh no!" E-Z cried as he ran toward the burning remains. "I have to find Uncle Sam and Samantha. I just have to."

His chair hovered over the remains; it was all charred black. An indistinguishable mess of destruction with no sign of human life. Sporadic items were soaked with water. Intermittent smoke signals rose here and there from among the extinguished embers.

E-Z raised his fists in the air. "Come here Eriel, you gargantuan-"

"Flying numpty!" Parker finished the insult.

Lia tried to calm everyone down.

"Why did you have to do it? Why? Why?" E-Z cried.

Lia fell to the ground. She rested her head on E-Z's knee and Parker hugged her just as a car squealed to a stop behind them.

Two doors flew open: Sam and Samantha.

They ran and clung together; like they'd never expected to see each other again. Everyone shed a tear or two, before they came apart. When they realized that the group hug included a man they didn't know.

The stranger was a tall man, who'd have no problem getting a spot on the Raptors. He was dressed from head to toe in a dark black pinstriped suit with matching shoes.

His jacket buttons unfastened revealed a black suit with a shiny fabric, possibly silk. His jet-black eyes and windswept locks contrasted with his ivy complexion. He resembled a cross between a mortician and a magician.

He held out his hand, "Hi, I'm Sam's insurance guy."

Uncle Sam explained that he and Samantha had gone out to get something to eat. Seeing E-Z's expression, he justified this, "She hadn't been able to sleep due to jet lag." Samantha and Sam exchanged glances, nodded. "Samantha and I…"

"Oh, Mom!"

E-Z said, "Samantha and Uncle Sam sitting in a tree – k-i-s-s-i-n-g."

"Stop," Parker said. "You're embarrassing them."

All eyes were directed at the insurance guy. His name was Reginald Oxworthy. He was on the phone. Shouting. "What do you mean he doesn't qualify?"

"Oh no!" Sam said.

"He's been our customer for years, first when he lived in another state and since moved here. He's covered, I'm certain of it." There was a pause. "Well, LOOK AGAIN!" He snapped his phone shut. "I'm sorry about all this."

Sam walked nearer and everyone else followed. "What exactly is the problem?"

"Oh, no problem so to speak."

"It sure sounded like a problem to me," Samantha said. The others nodded.

Oxworthy cleared his throat. "I told them to check your policy again. Give me a," his phone rang. "One sec," he said, walking away from them. They followed him like a group of footballers in a huddle, listening to every word he said. "Uh, yes. Righto. They've confirmed it then. No problem, it happens."

He beamed a smile in Sam's direction then gave him the thumbs up. He moved away from the entourage and continued his conversation.

They stood in a clump, looking at what remained of their home. A home which E-Z had lived in for his entire life. What would happen now? Would they have to rebuild on this location? A new house, with no history or meaning. A new house that would never be a home for him. Would never be a place where the ghosts of his parents, if ghosts existed, could visit.

Oxworthy made his way toward them. "Well, now. I do apologize for the delay. But your hotel reservations have been confirmed. We can get going. Settle you in, whenever you're ready."

"Thank you," Sam said. "Any idea yet, what was the cause of the fire?"

"After a preliminary investigation they are ninety percent certain the explosion was caused by a gas leak. But don't worry about that now. Your policy covers all costs for the hotel stay. I've booked you three rooms. That should suffice, shouldn't it?"

"That should be fine," Sam said. "Thank you, Reg."

"Your policy also covers expenses, for replacement items, necessities, food. You won't have to pay a cent at the hotel. Anything purchases, send me receipts. Make copies, you keep the originals. I'll see to it that you're reimbursed."

Sam and Oxworthy shook hands.

"Anyone need a lift to the hotel?" Oxworthy asked, and Lia and Samantha climbed into the backseat of his black Mercedes.

E-Z and Parker got into Uncle Sam's car.

"I don't think we've been introduced," Uncle Sam said, extending his hand to Parker who was in the back seat.

"Happy to meet you," Parker said.

"Oh, you're British too," Uncle Sam said. "Speaking of which, where's Alfred?"

E-Z shook his head. "I'll explain in the morning. And you can continue what you were going to tell us, about you and Samantha."

"Fair enough," Sam said, looking into his rear-view mirror to see Parker was sound asleep. He turned the car on and sped away.

"We've all had quite an eventful day," E-Z said.

"You're telling me."

Sorry Eriel, for blaming this on you, E-Z thought. Although an inkling in the back of his mind suggested the jury was still out on the matter.

CHAPTER TWENTY-TWO

Once everyone arrived at the hotel, they checked into their rooms, with a plan to meet later for dinner at 6 p.m.

Uncle Sam had a room to himself, but between his room and his nephew's they had an adjoining door. Parker was bunking in E-Z's room too, while Lia and her mother shared a room a few doors down.

After settling in, Lia and Samantha decided to shop for necessaries. Top priority was new clothes as everything they'd brought with them was lost in the fire.

"What about our passports?" Lia asked.

"Good thing I always keep them with me in my purse."

"Whew!" The two went into a designer store and immediately started trying on the latest North American fashions.

"This should be extra fun since the insurance company pays for everything!" Samantha exclaimed through the wall to her daughter in the adjoining change room.

"Nothing we love more than a shopping spree!" Lia said. "I'm definitely getting this, and this and this."

Back at the hotel, Parker was snoring away on the bed. E-Z was wheeling up and down the room thinking about his lost computer. Good thing he hadn't made it too far on his novel Tattoo Angel, but what was on his mind the most, were his parents' things. He couldn't believe they were all – GONE. It didn't help that he hadn't looked at them for an awfully long time. But why was he blaming himself? The insurance people said the cause was a gas leak. They said they were ninety percent certain. Why did he keep feeling that it was all his fault because he could have stopped it, stopped Eriel when he had the chance.

Sam poked his head into the room. "You two decent?"

Parker stretched.

"Yeah, we're decent. Come on in."

"I'm off down to the shops to get some essentials. You two want to give me a list of what you need, or do you want to join me?"

"If this involves food – count me in!" Alfred said.

"You're always hungry!"

"What can I say, I've been partaking of only grass for quite a while now."

E-Z caught Sam's look and pretended to smoke an imaginary cigarette.

Uncle Sam scoffed, wondering how his nephew at thirteen knew of such things. To change the subject, they locked their rooms and made their way down the hall.

"Where are we going exactly?" E-Z asked.

"That's right, we don't go shopping in the city very often. There's a fantastic mall, I've been wanting to go to since I moved here. It's not far, so I thought we could chat along the way."

"Can you tell us what happened?" Parker asked.

"Yeah, how did you and Samantha hook up so quickly?" E-Z asked.

"Hmmm," Sam said.

"I meant the fire," Parker said, giving E-Z a crossed eyed look over his shoulder.

They arrived at the store. Parker and Sam went in through the revolving doors, while E-Z used the door opener button to enter.

Once inside Parker bent down to retie his shoes. E-Z pulled a smart denim jacket off the clothes hanger and tried it on. He wheeled himself in front of a mirror to check out the fit. "This looks pretty good."

Sam came over to assess the situation, "Agreed, it's a precise fit. Looks like it was made for you."

"What do you think, Alfred?"

Sam did a double take. Parker said, "Would you quit calling me Alfred! Who was this Alfred guy anyway?"

"Uh, sorry it's the British accent. He had one too. Alfred was, well, a friend of ours."

Sam went back to looking at clothes. He was filling up a basket with underwear and toiletries.

"What do you think Parker?"

He crossed the floor to take a closer look. "It's a good fit. I think you should get it. But it'll be a shame when your wings bust out and it gets ruined."

Sam walked by and E-Z tossed the jacket into his basket. "I think you guys should get some necessaries, too, like undies. Unless you intend to go commando."

"Eww!" E-Z exclaimed.

"Oh, I'm familiar with that phrase. It's origin, I'm quite certain is in the UK."

"I can see why my nephew keeps calling you Alfred. That's the kind of thing he would have said."

E-Z glared at Parker for a second. Then followed his uncle on the way to the register where he stopped, tried on a hat, and tossed it into the basket.

"Now, where did Parker get to?" he asked. Sam continued looking at tie pins while E-Z scanned the store for his missing friend.

Parker stood stock still in the middle of Aisle Four with his right arm up, and his left arm down. The expression on his face was unmistakably zombie-like.

"Oh, no!" E-Z said as he wheeled over. "Uh, Parker," he whispered. "What's the matter? You better watch out or someone is going to confuse you with a mannequin."

Parker remained stock still.

"Snap out of it," E-Z said, knocking into Parker with his chair. Parker's body, tilted, then toppled over. E-Z grabbed him just in time, holding him up by the back of his shirt. He tried to straighten his friend up, so he didn't look so stiff and mannequin-like, but it wasn't an easy task.

Uncle Sam rushed over to help. "What's with Parker?"

"I don't know. We need to get him out of here."

"Does he take drugs? He has a weird expression on his face, like he's seen a ghost or something."

"No, no drugs, other than a little weed now and then. And there's no such things as ghosts – not to mention it's daytime. Maybe I can transport him on my chair? We've got to get him out of here before someone notices and calls the police.

"Agreed. I don't know what reason they'd give the police if they called them. There's a guy in our store who is imitating a mannequin! Come quick."

"Funny," E-Z said. "You go and check out and I'll stay here. Let's think of how we can get him out of here without drawing too much attention."

Uncle Sam went to pay while E-Z remained with Parker. Customers coming up the aisle, had problems getting in and around them. E-Z wheeled his chair left, then right, to accommodate the shoppers.

In the end, when there were several customers at once, he pushed Parker up against a wall. He was out of the way at least. Then sat waiting for Sam.

"We're over here!" E-Z called out when he spotted him.

"Why's he facing the wall? And what are you doing way over here?"

"There were lots of customers, and we were in the way. Did you think of how we can get him out of here?"

"Yes, I'm going to get one of those flatbeds," Sam said.

"Why not get a cart?" E-Z asked. "Less conspicuous."

"We'd never be able to get him into a cart. Not unless you want to break out your wings, pick him up and drop him into it."

"I need to think." After a few minutes, he realized getting a flatbed was the best idea. "Yes, get a flatbed and I can help you put him in it. Once we're out of the store, I can fly him back to the hotel. Only problem will be, when I get there, what to do with him then."

"We'll figure that out once we get out of the store." Sam went to get a cart. Instead, he returned with a flatbed. It turned out to be a better option. They easily got Parker onto it and headed back to the hotel.

"Let's walk back, slow and steady," E-Z said. "I don't need to fly after all. We'll take it nice and easy, go up to our room, put him onto his bed."

"Then I'll return the flatbed, I had to promise I'd personally return it."

"Sounds like a plan. Oops."

A group of shoppers were taking up most of the sidewalk. They stopped, to let them through, then continued their way again and were soon back at the hotel.

Once inside, the flatbed wouldn't fit on the normal elevator, so they had to use the service elevator. That took some convincing, i.e., bribing of the Concierge. Once the money changed palms, he even helped them to get the flatbed out of the elevator. He also offered to return it to the store when they were finished. An offer which Sam politely refused.

Now, outside of E-Z and Parker's room, the elevator opened and out stepped Lia and her mother. Each were carrying numerous bags when they noticed the guys and the flatbed.

"Oh, no! What happened?! Lia asked.

"Don't know," E-Z said. "He took a funny turn."

"Let's get him inside," Sam said.

After they put down their bags, the girls helped E-Z and Sam get Parker onto the bed.

"Maybe he's under a spell?" Lia suggested.

"That's a rather strange jump for you to make," Samantha said. "You've been watching way too many reruns of *Charmed.*"

Lia laughed. "Yes, it was one of my favourites. I mean the previous version the one with the girl from *Who's the Boss.*"

"Good to know you watch the oldies channel in the Netherlands too," E-Z said. Then he moved closer to Parker. "Wait a minute. Is he still breathing?"

They watched for the rise and the fall of Parker's chest. It didn't happen.

"Check for a heartbeat – or a pulse," Samantha suggested.

"There's a heartbeat," Sam said. "And he's breathing, but it's sporadic."

Samantha leaned over and felt Parker's forehead. "Oh, my, he's burning up with fever!"

"Get some ice!" Sam cried, then following his own order, ran out into the corridor with the ice bucket in tow.

"Shouldn't we call a doctor?" Samantha asked.

CHAPTER TWENTY-THREE

"I AGREE WITH MOM. We need to call an ambulance, or maybe the hotel has a doctor staying here," Lia said.

E-Z grimaced, ESPing Lia the message – we need to get rid of Uncle Sam and your mom.

Sam returned, with a bucketful of ice. "We need to get him into the bathtub." He and Samantha started lifting Parker.

"Wait!" Lia said. "Uh, Sam and Mom, why don't the two of you go and get lots and lots of ice? I mean, we need to fill the bathtub before we put him into it, right?"

"Uh, I think they're trying to get rid of us," Sam said.

"Sorry," E-Z said. "Can you give us a few minutes to try to figure this Parker situation out?"

Samantha and Sam nodded, then left the room.

E-Z recited the magic words which summoned Eriel:

Roch-Ah-Or, A, Ra-Du, EE, El.

Still the archangel did not appear. That he was being ignored annoyed E-Z to no end now that he knew he was being constantly monitored by Eriel.

Lia tried Haniel but received no reply.

E-Z and Lia did not know what to do when Parker's heart slowed in its beating and nearly came to a full stop.

Without being summoned or with fanfare, Ariel arrived. She flew straight over to Parker. She placed her hands upon his forehead. They watched as teardrops fell from her eyes and landed on his cheeks. She chanted, singing a soft song, and waited. When he did not move or regain consciousness she turned to depart. But before she went, she lamented, "He's gone." And seconds later so was she.

Even though they were on the 45th floor and even though Alfred/Parker was dead. Again. E-Z lifted him up from the bed and carried him to the window. He glanced back at Lia over his shoulder.

She was crying as he and Parker dropped.

Falling, falling. Until E-Z's wheelchair wings came out. Off they flew, he and Alfred, he, and Parker. They were both the same. Two for the price of one.

He was becoming delirious, as he rose higher and higher. The metal parts of his chair grew increasingly hot.

He feared they'd self-combust.

He had to make this right. He simply had to. He had to find Eriel.

The wheelchair began to convulse, causing E-Z and Alfred/Parker to fall.

They landed chair-less in the silo where E-Z clung to his friend's lifeless body.

It wasn't long until Eriel arrived and suspended in mid-air in front of them called out, "I told you it would happen. I told you and he agreed. The deal was done."

E-Z knew this to be true, and yet. "Why did you give him hope then, and why the Shakespeare quote about giving him a second chance?"

Eriel looked at the limp body which E-Z was holding. "That was not my doing."

"Then who do I need to speak with?" E-Z asked. "Bring him to me. God, or whoever's in charge. I demand to see him!"

CHAPTER TWENTY-FOUR

ERIEL HUFFED, THEN DISAPPEARED.

E-Z and Alfred/Parker remained. The name Parker was nothing and no one to him. Alfred was his friend and now that he was gone, he was going to remember him as Alfred and only Alfred.

Waiting for something and nothing all at the same time. E-Z cradled his dead friend's form, wishing him back to life again.

"Would you like a beverage?" the voice in the wall asked.

"I'd like my friend to be alive again. Can you bring him back to life again? Can you please help me to save him?"

"Please remain seated."

PFFT.

The soothing scent of lavender filled the air. He drifted off, into a dreamlike state where he was reliving a memory, a memory which had shifted and changed to suit his current situation.

There they were E-Z's mother and father alive and well, but younger. They were returning from the hospital in a car he'd never seen before. His father, Martin rushed out of the driver's seat, to help his mother, Laurel out of the car.

And together, they reached into the backseat and lifted out an infant seat. They looked lovingly at the baby in it, who was sound asleep.

"He's like his big brother," Martin said.

"Yes, E-Z always fell asleep in the car," Laurel said.

"Come on inside," Martin cooed.

"And meet your big brother," Laurel said, as the infant opened his eyes briefly then went back to sleep again.

E-Z who'd been looking out the window, with his Uncle Sam beside him. Wanting to go outside and greet his new baby brother or sister.

"Wait for them to come inside," Uncle Sam said.

"Okay," seven-year-old E-Z said, with his face pushed against the window cradled in his two hands.

The front door opened, "We're home!" his mother Laurel called.

E-Z ran to the front door, where his mother and father hugged him. They squatted down to present the newest member of the Dickens family.

"It's so small," E-Z said.

"He's a he," his father said.

"Oh."

"Would you like to hold him?" his mother asked.

"Okay," E-Z said, holding his arms so his mother could place his little brother into it. "I don't want to wake him up though. Would he mind?"

"No, he won't wake up," Laurel said.

"If he does, it's because he wants to meet his big brother."

"Does he have a name?" E-Z asked, taking the newborn into his arms, and cradling his head.

"Not yet, would you like to name him?" his mother asked. "Good, hold his neck, just so...very good. How did you know to do that? You're such a good big brother."

"Great job, buddy," his dad said.

E-Z looked down into the cygnet's face and said, "He looks like an Alfred to me."

Tears rolled down E-Z's cheeks as the two worlds collided. In one he cradled his baby brother named Alfred. In the other he cradled Alfred's dead body in the silo.

"Wait time is now seven minutes," the voice in the wall said.

"Seven minutes," E-Z repeated.

He thought about Alfred, about his powers. About how he could heal other life forms, including humans. He was wondering if Alfred, had healed the young man. Had done the switch himself? Would that have been possible?

"Alfred," E-Z said. "Alfred, can you hear me?" He shook his friend's body. "Alfred!" he said, over and over again hoping his friend could hear him somehow.

As the wall's clock counted down, Ariel appeared. "You cannot treat the body, in such a way. It is a disgrace." She spread her wings and went to lift Alfred's limp body out of E-Z's arms with the intention of taking it away.

"No!" E-Z said. "You shall not have him."

Ariel shook her wings, then her index finger at E-Z.

"Alfred has left the building, you are holding the skin, the suit which held him. Alfred is where he is meant to be now. Let his body go."

E-Z sat up. If Alfred was with his family somewhere, if that was true, then yes, he could let him go. Until then he was holding on.

"Where is he exactly? Is he with his family?"

Ariel fluttered close, remarkably close, nearly sitting on E-Z's nose. "That I cannot say."

"Then I am not letting him go."

"Fine," Ariel said. She huffed and disappeared.

Above him, in the silo appeared two figures a man and a woman. They moved toward him and floated down. Nearer and nearer.

He rubbed his eyes. Was he dreaming again? It was his mother and his father. Martin and Laurel. Angels, coming to greet him. He shook his head. It couldn't be them. It couldn't be. He'd been dreaming of them – them bringing home a baby brother. Now they were here, with him in the silo. As clear as day – but was he still sleeping? Dreaming?

"E-Z," his mother said. "This person, your friend Alfred is dead. You must let him go and continue with your work. You must complete the trials and the clock is ticking. You are running out of time."

E-Z's father Martin said, "It's the only way we can all be together again."

"But they lied to him," E-Z said. "They told him that he would be with his family. He can't be with his family now, not like this. How do I know they're not lying to me, about being with you? How do I know that you're not a manipulation by Eriel to get me to do his bidding?"

"Who is Eriel?" his mother asked.

"We don't know Eriel," his father said.

This made no sense. This was Eriel's place. Whether they knew him or not didn't matter, he was responsible for them being there. He knew how-to pull-on E-Z's heartstrings. He knew how to how to get him to do what he wanted him to do.

What exactly did he want? And why was he using his parents to get it? It was shameless. In the air above him, his parents hovered, turning their smiles on and off like they were puppets. That was when he knew for certain the two ghosts, or whatever they were, weren't his parents after all. They were figments of his imagination, or possibly of Eriel's. What he couldn't figure out was why. Why was he being so cruelly and shamelessly manipulated?

"Wake up E-Z!"

He was back in his bed. In his house.

He rolled over and went back to sleep...and landed back in the silo - again.

CHAPTER TWENTY-FIVE

THREE SILO-LIKE THINGS FLOATED around the room like they were playing a game of Follow the Leader.

They were not silos. They were authentic eternal resting places called Soul Catchers.

Every time a living thing perished, provided the body in which it lived had been born with a soul, would one day live on. The Soul Catchers were many, too numerous to count. Their numbers were far greater than we humans can comprehend. More than a googolplex, which is the biggest known number.

When E-Z arrived, as before he was deposited into his waiting soul catcher.

Alfred arrived next, still dead his body was placed into his soul catcher.

Lia arrived last, still asleep into her soul catcher.

It didn't take long for E-Z to start to feel claustrophobic.

"Would you like a beverage?" the voice in the wall asked.

"No thank you," he said, drumming his fingers on the arm of his wheelchair, when an angel appeared. A new angel, one he hadn't seen before.

This angel was a woman. She was dressed in a flowing black gown and cap – like she was participating in a graduation ceremony. On her stern looking face, was a pair of glasses. Similar to the ones Marilyn Monroe wore on the poster at the Café. The difference was these frames pulsed with red liquid which resembled blood.

"E-Z," she said, in a quakingly loud voice. Her voice reverberated. "Welcome back to your Soul Catcher."

"Soul Catcher?" he said. "Is that what this thing is called? To me it looks more like a silo. So, what's a Soul Catcher anyway?"

"It's an eternal resting place for souls," she said, like she'd answered the same question a million times before.

"But isn't that for when people are dead? I'm not dead." He sure hoped he wasn't dead!

"Wait!" she shouted.

Again, she shook the walls when she talked. And his teeth vibrated too. So much so that his preference would be outside in the snow, then having to hear her utter another word.

"I didn't tell you this was question and answer time. As I see it, you have completed most of your trials successfully. Albeit Alfred assisted in trial number two. As you know unsanctioned assistance is not allowed."

E-Z opened his mouth to defend Alfred, but only closed it again. He didn't want to risk her raising her voice again. He sure wished they'd turn up the heat in there. Then again, it was a place for souls. Maybe souls preferred cold storage.

TICK-TOCK.

A blanket was now draped around his shoulders.

"Thank you."

"You are right when you die your soul will rest here. Or would have rested here, had we let you die. But we kept you alive. We had good reason to do so. Things have changed though. It hasn't worked out. Therefore, we'd like to rescind our original deal."

"What do you mean rescind it? You've got some nerve! Trying to cancel an agreement, what is it just because I'm a kid? There are laws against child labour. Besides, I've done everything asked of me. Sure, I've had to learn it all on the fly. But through thick and thin I've done it. I've kept my end of the bargain, and you should keep yours!"

"Oh yes, you have done what's been asked of you. That's the problem – you lack initiative."

"Lack initiative!" E-Z exclaimed as he smashed his fists down on the arms of his wheelchair. "The agreement was you send me trials and I figure out how to conquer them. I've saved lives. You can't change the rules halfway through the game."

"True, that was the original agreement. Then things went wrong with Hadz and Reiki – they forgot to wipe minds – for one thing and Eriel had to get involved."

"He sent me trials, I completed them. I even beat him in a duel."

"Yes, you did. I'd asked him to assess the bonds between you and your Uncle Sam."

"To evaluate us?"

"Yes. An archangel isn't meant to CREATE trials for an angel in training. Due to your, well, lack of initiative, Eriel had to get more involved than he should have been."

"Wait just a minute! So, you're saying I was meant to go out and find my own trials? Why didn't anyone fill me in on these requirements?"

"We hoped you'd figure it out for yourself. There have been clues. Clues about the big picture. Commonalities. We hoped if you had others to discuss the trials with. The trials you've already completed. That you'd zero in on the problem. Come to the same conclusion.

Help us out. Maybe even conquer it – without us having to spoon feed it to you. We gave you every opportunity, but you didn't do it. So, we're going another way."

"Commonalities? I might know what you mean."

"If you figure it out and take the Superhero option...That would work. So long as everything was crystal clear. You had the full picture. Knew the risks."

"So, we'll still be a team? Why don't you spell it out? Make it easy for me?"

"In the past, even though your companions were given powers, which you did not possess – you didn't utilize them. Instead, the three of you sat around – wasting time – waiting for everything to happen.

Didn't you think it odd when Eriel appeared in the amusement park? He was raising *The Three's* profiles. That's not an archangel's job. It's your job."

He shook his head. "I wasn't one hundred percent certain it was Eriel, until he identified himself at the end. Before that I had my suspicions. Who else would dress like Abraham Lincoln?

"Besides, I thought no one was meant to know. Up to that point, I thought the trials were secrets. I was afraid of breaking my agreement with you. Ophaniel said if I told anyone, I'd lose the chance to see my parents again. I followed the rules set out for me. I don't think you understand the concept of fair play."

"This isn't a game. Archangels can do whatever we want to do!" she exclaimed, moving closer to where E-Z was seated. She thrust her chin forward. "We decided you were more suited to the Superhero game than the Angel game. It was then, you were assisted in the PR department. To encourage you to find your own people to help. God knows the earth is full of them. What did Shakespeare call them, those who are mewling and puking in their nurse's arms."

"I haven't read any Shakespeare, but I'm related to Charles Dickens. Not that it's relevant. But, okay, so, you want me to continue, as a Superhero with Alfred, if he lives and with Lia by my side. We can easily get lots of support and publicity from the media.

"I'm still committed to you. If you'll allow us free reign, why, the sky will be the limit. We know lots of kids at school and in the sports industry. We can set up a Superhero Hotline, and a website. We can use social media to connect with people from all over the world. People will be lining up for us to help them. It'll be a whole new ballgame."

"Ah, at last he speaks of initiative...but my dear boy it's way too little too late. As I said before, we want out of the obligation to you. You are no longer bound to us. You no longer have a debt to pay."

"But..."

"All three of you have proven that you are only in this for yourselves. When the angels first suggested you could help us, represent us here on earth – we had a plan. With Alfred, it was the same. Then, Lia came along. Since then, we've had some success with the two of you. We included her in the trio...but now you've been rendered obsolete."

"We save people, we help people."

"Don't give me that. If I offered you the chance to be with your parents today, here, and now. You'd throw in the towel. Off you'd go without a care or thought for those lives you might have saved had the trials continued.

"Same with Alfred, I expect – that's if he survives. He'd be off in a field of daisies with his family without a blink of an eye. And speaking of eyes if Lia had her sight back – she'd be off too.

"After careful consideration we realized none of you are committed to anything other than yourselves, hence, we have moved on to Plan B."

"Wait a minute. Let's define work." He googled it and was pleased to find he had four bars. "According to an online dictionary: to perform work or fulfill duties regularly for wages or salary. I worked for you, without payment. Other than a promise of compensation. We had a verbal agreement.

"I'm not sure of the details of what deal Alfred had, or Lia, but I bet their angels offered them similar incentives. I kept my end of the bargain, and you should keep to yours. I'm thirteen years old and," he googled it. "Yes, as I thought according to the US Department of Labour, fourteen is the minimum work age."

She laughed and readjusted her glasses. He noticed she had blood on her hands. She wiped them on her black garment. "Early laws are not applicable to angels or archangels. It's naïve for you to think it would be though." She paused. "We are prepared to offer you two choices. Option number one: You will remain here in your Soul Catcher for the rest of your life."

"What?"

The very foundations of his Soul Catcher quaked. The idea of being buried alive inside this metal container sickened him.

"The life you will live, for your living breathing days will be spent as promised by those imbecile archangels. With your parents. That is, you will re-live your life with your parents from the day you were born up until the exact moment when their lives expired. You'd never be in a wheelchair, and they would never die." She paused. "Now, you may speak."

"Do you mean I'll re-live my life with my parents, every single day we had together, for all eternity, over and over again?"

"Yes."

"What's option number two?"

"Can't you guess?" she asked with a toothy smirk.

Her smile was insincere that he had to look away.

He waited.

"Option two would mean you go back to live your life with your Uncle Sam." She hesitated, moving closer so E-Z. He was already cold, and now she was making him even colder with every flap of her wings. He covered himself with the blanket. She continued. "As you might have already guessed, you will not, nor ever will be reunited with your parents with either option. We'd recreate the past. It would be like you'd be living in a play or television show."

"What! That is not what I agreed to!" E-Z exclaimed. "Are your saying Hadz. Reiki, Eriel and Ophaniel lied to me?"

"Lied is a strong word, but yes. Look at your surroundings. Souls are deposited into individual compartments. A compartment is prepared in advance for each soul."

"So, you're saying my parents are each in one of these things?"

"Yes, their souls are."

"And then what happens to them?"

"Why, they float around in the heavens."

"That's sad. I always thought my parents would be together, somewhere. I know that was the only thing which gave Alfred some kind of solace. That his wife and kids were together somewhere. No one likes to think of their loved one dying alone. Let alone spending eternity inside a metal container drifting around from place to place."

"Human sentimentality. Souls merely exist. They do not live and breathe, nor do they eat, or feel too hot or too cold. Humans don't understand the concept."

He scoffed.

"I don't mean to insult your species. But when a body expires, what remains, the soul, is a difficult concept to wrap your mind around. Human brains are just too small to comprehend the complexities of the universe. Hence the creation of religious doctrines. Written in layman's terms. Easy to be taught and followed without any proof."

"Since souls are more valued than humans like me, how could I live the rest of my life in one of these containers?"

"We have made adjustments, like now and before. You had no problems existing in here when we brought you in, now did you?"

"Other than claustrophobia," he said. "And the times when they needed to calm me down with that lavender spray."

"Ah, yes. The recurrence of claustrophobia will of course be dependent upon which option you choose. If you choose Option number one, the environment will sustain you in all ways until your soul is ready. Then your earthly form can be disposed of. Humans adapt, and you'd get used to it. Plus, you'll be with your parents, reliving memories. This will pass the time. Now, name your choice!"

"Wait, what about my wings, and my chair's wings? What will happen to them?" He hesitated, "What about Alfred and Lia's powers? If we choose option number one, will we go back to the way we would have been? I mean before you and the other archangels became involved in our lives?"

"Of course, we're not going to pull off your wings, my dear boy, or remove any powers any of you have already been given. We're archangels, not sadists."

"Good to know, so, we can continue being Superheroes."

"You can, but you'll have to create your own publicity – because when we're out – we're out for good."

"Please remain seated," the voice in the wall said, although E-Z didn't have much choice in the matter.

The archangel said nothing. Instead, she distracted herself by cleaning her glasses then putting them back on again.

"One more thing," E-Z asked, "concerning Alfred."

"Go on but do hurry it up. Another concept humans don't get, is that time exists throughout the universe. I do have other places to be and other archangels to see."

"Alright, I'll get to it. Alfred is now in another human body. If the soul remains with the body, then, are two souls in there? Is the soul catcher waiting for two souls?"

The angel turned her back on him. She cleared her throat before speaking, "I, we, were hoping you wouldn't ask that question. You're smarter than we anticipated." She closed her eyes, nodded, "Mhmmm." Her eyes remained closed. E-Z looked to see if she was wearing earplugs as she appeared to be listening to someone. Or maybe he was imagining it. She nodded. "Agreed," she said.

"Is someone else in here with us?" he asked.

A new voice boomed from all around him. Why did all archangels have such loud voices?

"I am Raziel the Keeper of Secrets. E-Z Dickens you must heed my words. For once they have been spoken, you shall not remember them. Nor that I was here. Soul Catchers and their purposes are not your concern. You've overstepped your boundaries, and we will not tolerate it! We've generously given you two options. Decide NOW, or my learned friend will make the decision for you."

E-Z started to speak, but then his mind went blank. What were they talking about?

The archangel closed her eyes again, mouthed the words, "Thank you," and Raziel's voice spoke no more.

It was like the time had jumped backwards. "You expect me to decide on the spot, without giving me time to think about it? Without talking to my Uncle Sam or to my friends? Speaking of which, what about Alfred, he was told he would be reunited with his family? And Lia, she was told she'd get her eyesight back."

"Since Alfred is gone, your decision – whether he survives on earth or not - will be his decision. His number one option will be the same as yours. Would he want to relive his life with his family repeatedly? As he's gone, he may already be having pleasant dreams about them. Then again, one never knows what tricks the mind can play. He may be in a loop of nightmares and only you can rescue him and his family by making the right choice for him."

"Are you saying he will never come out of it? For definite?"

"That I can't say. All I know is, the soul catcher is not ready to collect his soul...yet."

"And Lia?"

"Her human eyes are gone in this life, like your legs are. She can relive her sighted days, but she may prefer for to you to choose for her too. After all, she hasn't had time to grow up and mature like a normal child would. She's already lost three years of her life and this aging episode, we're not sure if it's a one off, or, if it will happen again."

"You mean, you don't know what is going to happen to her either?"

"No, we don't. Besides, she's still sleeping."

"I can't decide this, for all three of us on a time limit. It's a big decision and I need time."

"Then you shall have it." A clock appeared, counting down from sixty minutes. "Your time starts now. Give me your answer before it hits zero. Otherwise, everything we have discussed will be invalid. And you'll find yourselves back at the hotel with your friend's dead body." Her wings flapped and she rose higher and higher.

"Wait, before you go," he cried.

"What is it now?"

"Are there others, I mean other kids like us?"

"It's been nice knowing you," she said.

"The feeling is definitely not mutual," he replied.

CHAPTER TWENTY-SIX

As the minutes ticked away, E-Z went over everything he'd just been told. He wished the silo was wide enough so he could move around more. At least he was sitting comfortably in his wheelchair. Together they were like the dynamic duo.

"Would you like something to eat?" the voice from the wall asked.

"Sure would," he said. "An apple, some popcorn – cheese flavoured would be good and a bottle of water."

"Coming right up," the voice said, as a metallic table pushed through a slit in the wall he hadn't noticed before. It came to rest in front of him. From the slit out came a hook, carrying first the bottle of water. Then a second hook carrying a glass. A third hook followed with an apple. Before setting it down, the hook polished it with a towel. Then a fourth hook popped out, carrying a bowl of popcorn.

"Thank you," he said as the four grasping hooks waved and disappeared back into the wall.

"You are welcome."

"Uh, any chance you could get my computer to me? It was destroyed in the fire. I'd sure like to be able to make a list of the things to make this decision."

"Sure thing. Just give me a minute or two."

As he was finishing up the apple and contemplating the popcorn, from another slot on the opposite wall his laptop appeared. The hook held it aloft, waiting for E-Z to move the other objects to accommodate it. When he didn't do so, hooks appeared from the other side. One picked up the apple core and disappeared back into the wall. Another poured the remaining water in the the glass. Then took the empty bottle back through the slot in the wall. Since he wanted to keep the the popcorn and the glass of water, he removed them from the table. The hook set down his laptop, then returned through its slot in the wall.

E-Z thought the hooks were cool accessories. He could easily market them to a big Swedish chain.

Now that the hooks were all gone, he lifted the lid of his laptop and clicked it on. First, he checked his Tattoo Angel file, everything was still there! He was so happy; he would have wept if the clock weren't ticking the time away.

"Thank you so much," he said, cramming a handful of cheesy popcorn into his mouth. And then he started typing. He decided to think about himself third. First, write down the pros and cons about Alfred. Straight off he knew Alfred wouldn't mind reliving his past with his family repeatedly. He would have gone for that option straightaway.

"Still, it seemed to E-Z that it wasn't an option his family would have wanted him to take. Since he'd be reliving what already was, not moving forward. In life, you're meant to move forward. To continuing learning and growing.

The more he thought about it, the more he realized it would be like binge-watching your life-story. Imagine your life twenty-four-seven on permanent loop. Never knowing when it would end. Or if it would ever end. That could turn into a different kind of hell. One he which didn't bear thinking about.

Except, if he knew for certain Alfred would always be in a coma. Which the archangel had alluded to. Then for him, making the choice would ward off any bad dreams or nightmares. Alfred would be with his family, forever. Even though it wasn't the real thing...it might be enough. Would he choose it?

He glanced at the time, fifty minutes left. He began to think of Lia's case. Her dream of becoming a famous ballerina had been cut short. Would she want to relive the childhood, knowing that dream would never be fulfilled? For her, it would be worth taking a chance on the future. The eyes in the palms of her hands made her special, unique...and she was likable. She might even be the latest version of a wonder woman, if she were able to harness all the powers.

"E-Z?" Lia said. "I can hear you thinking, but where are you?"

Oh no! Now she was awake he'd have to explain everything to her, and it would take time and time was running out. He'd have to do it, quickly. "Listen Lia," he began, "I have a long tale to tell you, please don't stop me until the tale is complete. We're running out of time." He explained it all, it took him ten minutes. Another ten minutes gone. Forty minutes remained.

"Okay, E-Z, you think about you, and I'll think about me. Let's take five minutes, then we'll talk again. Time starts now."

"Good plan."

Five minutes later and the clock showed thirty-five minutes remaining. E-Z asked Lia if she had decided.

"I have," she said. "What about you?"

"Me too," he said. "You first, in five minutes or less if you can."

"It comes down to a pretty easy decision for me, E-Z. I don't want to stay in this thing and live my life here. When the Soul Catcher brings me here when I'm dead. That's fine. But I don't want to be forcefully confined to this space. Not when I could be out there feeling the warmth of the sunshine, listening to the birds, with the wind in my hair. Not to mention spending time with my mom and with Uncle Sam, and hopefully you. Life's too short to waste and I like my new eyes most of the time." She laughed.

"I agree and if I were you, I'd do the same."

"Thanks, E-Z. What time is left now?"

"Twenty-five more minutes," he confirmed. "Now here's my thinking in hopefully less than five minutes. I don't mind it in here, it's not much different than being out there. I've learned that in a wheelchair isn't the end of the world. In fact, I've grown quite used to it. I can do things I used to do before like play baseball, and I don't totally suck at it. Heck, they'll even play it at the Paralympics.

"My parents wouldn't want me to waste my life living in the past. Nor would Uncle Sam. I'm not willing to give everything up, just because those twit archangels made a few unseemly promises. So, I agree with you. We're getting the heck out of these Soul Catcher things. We'll live our lives until we're finished living. And then it can good and proper come and catch us. Years later, after hopefully we'll have contributed to mankind and led good lives. We could find others like us. We could set up a Superhero hotline and work together all over the world. We could use our powers, to make the world a better place. We could live our lives to the fullest; create inspiring lives we'd be proud of, and our families wou ld too."

"Bravo!" Lia exclaimed. "But are there others, like us?"

"I asked the angel who explained everything to me, but she didn't answer. That makes me think that there are." He glanced at the clock. "Only twenty-one minutes left."

"What about Alfred? Will he ever wake up?"

"The angel said she didn't know, only the soul catcher knows...but she did say he might be having nightmares. If there's a chance, he's in a living hell, then we better let him go. Option number one, him reliving life with his family on loop is the one for him?"

"I disagree. Not one of us knows for certain, when the soul catcher will come for us. Alfred wouldn't want to waste away in here because bad dreams might find him. Not where there's a chance, he could help someone or inspire someone. We came in here together and we should leave here together. In my opinion, that's that."

Fourteen minutes and ticking.

She'd gone at Alfred's issue in a unique way Was she right? Would Alfred indeed, wish to give up his family in this scenario for an unchartered future? Don't we all exist in an unchartered world? Changing courses, ducking, and diving. Opening windows, closing doors. Letting our emotions lead us astray and then back again. It's all about living. Yes, Lia was right. It was a done deal.

Eight minutes left on the clock.

"I think you're right, Lia. It's all for one and one for all," E-Z said. "The archangel told me I needed to speak the words before the clock ran out. Then we'd all find ourselves back in the hotel...like this Soul Catcher interlude never happened."

"Do you think we'll still remember about the soul catchers, though? It's an important thing for us to learn from this experience. Even if we didn't share it. Keep in mind that it blows apart everything we know about heaven and the afterlife."

Five minutes left.

"It does, but let's discuss this on the other side." He clenched his fists as the clock ticked down to four minutes. "We've decided!" he shouted. "Get the three of us out of these, these soul catchers – NOW!"

The walls of E-Z's silo began to shake. "Are you okay, Lia?" he shouted. She didn't reply. The ground under his feet seemed to rattle and rumble. Then it started turning, clockwise first, then counterclockwise, then clockwise.

Inside his stomach twisted. He spewed out cheesy popcorn and chewed red apple bits everywhere.

They were the only souvenirs the Soul Catcher would have of him. Hopefully for an awfully long time.

Acknowledgments

Dear Readers,

Thank you for reading the second book in the E-Z Dickens Series. I hope you like the addition of these new characters and are keen to find out what happens next. Which you can do right now as the 3rd and 4th books are currently available.

Thank you once again to my beta readers, proof readers and editors. Your advice and encouragement kept me on track with this project and your input was/is always appreciated.

Thank you also to family and friends for always being there for me.

And as always, Happy Reading!

Cathy

About The Author

Cathy McGough lives and writes in Ontario, Canada with her husband, son, their two cats and one dog.

Also By:

FICTION

YA

E-Z Dickens Superhero Book Three: Red Room

E-Z Dickens Superhero Book Four: On Ice

NON-FICTION

103 Fundraising Ideas For Parent Volunteers With Schools and Teams (3RD PLACE BEST REFERENCE 2016 METAMORPH PUBLISHING)